FIRST ORIGINAL

Copyright ©

All rights reserved. No pa
any form or by any mea   ... consent from the
author.

This is a work of fiction. Names, characters, places and incidents either are the product of the author's imagination or are used factiously. Any resemblance to actual person's, living or dead, events, or locales are entirely coincidental.

ISBN-13: 978-1977772305
ISBN-10: 1977772307
eBook ISBN: 9781926440477

Book & cover design by Wolf & Eagle Media
Cover image by vishstudio

www.deborahbladon.com

Also by Deborah Bladon

THE OBSESSED SERIES
THE EXPOSED SERIES
THE PULSE SERIES
THE VAIN SERIES
THE RUIN SERIES
IMPULSE
SOLO
THE GONE SERIES
FUSE
THE TRACE SERIES
CHANCE
THE EMBER SERIES
THE RISE SERIES
HAZE
SHIVER
TORN
THE HEAT SERIES
MELT
THE TENSE DUET
SWEAT

Chapter 1

Crew

There are certain luxuries afforded a man when he owns a club in Manhattan. He can drink the best scotch in the world and expense that shit. He can pick a different woman every night of the week, and he can sit on his ass and watch one of his best friends get hit on by some schmuck in a suit that's two sizes too big or he can do something about it.

I've had my fill of scotch tonight and the woman I was with last night is waiting for me back at her place. I can't leave my club, Veil East, yet. That's because, Adley York, one of my closest friends is about to go home with a professional baseball player with a reputation for hitting it out of the park.

It doesn't matter to me if another man is stellar in bed. I don't compare myself to anyone. I've never had a complaint in all the years I've been active on the Manhattan social scene. I have zero doubt that I've fucked more women than Trey Hale, but by the look of what's happening on the dance floor, he's about to take Adley home to screw her.

That is not happening on my watch.

I can't have her because there are women that you friend and women that you fuck. Adley falls squarely in the first category although my traitorous cock wants her in the second. It can't happen. If I take that petite blonde to bed, I'll lose her, and the hole

TROUBLEMAKER   *Deborah Bladon*

that would leave in my life is something I don't have the fucking emotional maturity to deal with.

"Adley," I call out her name over the booming beat that vibrates off the walls. Why the hell did I have a state of the art sound system installed in this place? "Hey, Ad."

By the grace of God, she notices me pointing at her. She tosses me a wave and a wiggle of her ass before she grabs hold of the star pitcher's shoulders. I swear to fuck if she climbs up on that right now, I'll haul her off the floor over my shoulder.

I motion for her to come to where I'm standing. Shaking her head, she flips me the bird.

I slam my now empty tumbler on the bar and stalk toward her.

"I need to talk to you." I stand next to her. "It's important, Adley."

"It can wait, Crew." Her pretty face flushes. "I'm a little busy right now."

She's a little drunk right now. I see it in her eyes and her hips. She's aching for some and if anyone is going to give it to her, it'll be me.

No. I fucking can't. Those perfect tits and that curvy ass are off-limits.

"I'm going to drop you off at your apartment." I take a quick look around. The club is running smoothly tonight. We're at full capacity. I don't need to be here to benefit from this. "Grab your stuff and let's go."

"Why would l do that?" Her eyes rake my six-foot-three, two-hundred-pound frame. The fact that my black button down shirt, matching pants, and

TROUBLEMAKER   *Deborah Bladon*

shoes are all designer labels doesn't impress Adley. It never has. "You're not as fun as Trey is."

Trey has nothing on me. I'm taller, richer, and a hell of a lot better looking than he is. I own a mirror. Black hair, green eyes and a smile that has never failed me to date are what I see every morning.

"You've had too much to drink, Ad."

"Maybe you haven't had enough." She pokes her finger into the center of my chest. "You work out."

Like a madman, every morning at five a.m. before the city wakes up. "We're leaving."

"What if I want to go with him?"

"Pick another night to make that happen." I direct that statement to Hale. "She's not going anywhere with you tonight."

"Who are you? Her husband?"

Adley laughs so hard she bends over revealing a perfect bird's eye view of the top of her round breasts. The decent thing to do is to look away, but I don't.

"I'm her friend. I own the club." I push a hand at him. "Crew Benton."

"You're Benton?" He steps closer and studies my face, his hand eagerly shaking mine. "Your reputation precedes you, man."

I have no idea what the fuck that means, so I steer him to a place I'll know he'll go. "Your drinks are on the house for the rest of the night. Tell Penny at the bar, Crew's got the tab."

"No shit?"

"No shit," I repeat back. "It's a limited time offer so..."

3

TROUBLEMAKER   *Deborah Bladon*

"Understood." He doesn't give Adley another look before he heads for the bar.

"That was a cock-block, a totally intentional cock-block." She frowns. "You ruined my night. Now, what am I supposed to do?"

I eye her up. Small black dress, hair so messed up that she looks like she just fucked in the back of a beat-up pickup truck and a mouth that was made for sin. "Come to my place, Adley. I want you to come home with me."

"What for?" She scrunches her button nose. "I already told you that I'm never going to sit through another episode of that show you like. You know I'm scared of dragons."

She did say that. She didn't mean it though. I know that just like I know virtually everything about her except what she looks and sounds like when she has an orgasm.

"Today's your lucky day." I glance over at Hale. He's still got his eyes locked tight on Adley's ass. "We're all caught up. The new season doesn't start for another six months."

"Then we don't need to talk about it now." She links her fingers together in front of her. "Besides, I don't want to leave yet. I'm having too much fun."

That's the reason I want her out of here. This is the first time I've been at the club when she's been here. She knows she never has to pay for a drink and she takes full advantage of that since we opened a year ago. I always glance at the amount of her tab when I take care of the comps at the end of each month.

TROUBLEMAKER   *Deborah Bladon*

Ad is on a very short-list of people I'll give free alcohol to. She's on an even shorter list of people I'll do virtually anything for including risking my own life to save theirs.

"I need your help." It's the first thing I can think of to say.

"Are you doing another one of those thousand-piece puzzles?" She steals a glance at Hale, along with a subtle wave of her fingers. "I tried to help you last time you took that on, but we both know how that ended."

The puzzle was an idea my friend Liam, a therapist, pressed on me last winter. He said it would help alleviate stress. He was dead wrong. Every single piece of that hard-as-fuck mind twister ended up being thrown against the wall of my apartment. Adley bore witness to that and she's never let me forget that a box of jagged-edge little pieces of cardboard got the better of me. She brings it up every chance she can.

I like that the memory is etched in the forefront of her mind. I know it's because she cares. She's the one who told me I needed to do something about my stress. She was right. That's where the early wake-up call to hit the gym fits into my life.

"I want to talk to you," I say because I can't tell her what I really want is to forget that we mutually agreed, soon after we met, to keep things platonic. "It's been a long day, Ad. I could use a friend."

"There are hundreds of people in this club." She surveys the packed dance floor. "You must have at least a dozen friends here. Why don't you have a

5

TROUBLEMAKER   *Deborah Bladon*

drink with one of them? I'm not in the mood to hang out."

"Why would I want to hang out with any of them?" Her fuck-me look is melting my brain cells one-by-one. I sound like a desperate sixteen-year-old kid who is trying to keep his crush away from his arch enemy. I shoot Hale a look. "You're the most interesting person I know. I want to run something by you."

"Something?" She repeats the word back with a curve of her lip. "Is about makeup? Do I get free samples?"

Of course she does. My day job is Chief Operating Officer at Matiz Cosmetics. I run the company in tandem with my closest friend Nolan Black. As fate would have it, Nolan married Ad's best friend, Ellie. That's how we met. "We're launching a new mascara line. I need your input. What are your thoughts on navy blue?"

"That would look killer on me." She bats her naturally long eyelashes. They frame the bluest eyes I've ever seen. They're dotted with faint specks of violet. I'm not even sure she realizes how unique her eyes are. "I told you six months ago that colored mascara was the way to go."

She did tell me that. I don't generally consult with veterinary assistants when it comes to future products for Matiz, but Ad is our target market and she's brutally honest. Those two things, among others, make her invaluable to me.

"I've got the samples for three different shades in my office." I smile inwardly. If I take her to the Matiz tower, I'll get my head in a different space. I

6

TROUBLEMAKER   *Deborah Bladon*

need that right now. I've been fighting this undeniable attraction to her for months and at this moment I'm losing the fucking battle. "We can head over there now."

She considers it before she glances one last time at Hale. "I gave him my number before you showed up. I hope to hell he uses it and calls me. He's so hot."

I want to go over and squeeze his phone in my palm until it's in pieces, but I won't. I can't control this. I have no claim on her. I wish my cock would see it that way.

"I feel lightheaded. Maybe I did have too much to drink." She grabs my forearm. "I'm starving. I could use a burger. Can we stop and get food? It's my treat."

I stare down at her.

Christ, woman. Please stop being everything I need.

I don't say that or anything else. Instead, I nod as I scoop her hand into mine. I can do this. I can keep it together for the rest of the night. I've done it for months. What's another hour or two?

Chapter 2

Crew

"A pierced nipple."
Jesus.
Those are three words I never thought I'd hear coming from Adley's lips, yet there they are.

I stand frozen behind her, a chocolate milkshake in my hand. She's talking on the phone to someone who I hope to hell isn't Trey Hale.

When her phone rang, I was already up and on my feet heading to the counter in this fast food place to pick up her forgotten shake. She ordered for us both and paid as promised. The first time I tried to talk her out of buying me dinner, she scoffed and explained that she always keeps it even between her and her friends.

It was yet another slap-to-the-side-of-the-head reminder that we're *just friends* and always will be.

"I need to go, Syd." Her voice softens as she says her roommate, Sydney's, nickname. "I'm going to hang with Crew for a few hours so do what you've got to do with Banner. I'll text before I get there."

I move forward when she places her phone back on the table. "I have one chocolate shake for the beauty queen with mustard on her chin."

She swipes the back of her hand over her chin. "Did I get it?"

I lower myself back into the chair I was in earlier. It's made of cheap plastic, the table is uneven and the food is close to the worst I've ever had, but

TROUBLEMAKER   *Deborah Bladon*

the company makes it worth it. I slide the straw from its paper wrapper before I stab it through the center of the lid that covers the shake. "You can use a napkin, Ad. That's why they supply them."

Her tongue lashes the back of her hand. "I'm not wasting any of this. I love the burgers here."

I don't concur, but I didn't have anything to eat since lunch, so I held my breath and chowed down on the cheeseburger and fries she bought me. I push the milkshake across the table until it's in front of her. "You're not feeling lightheaded anymore, are you?"

She shakes her head. "I'm fine. Did you hear what I was talking to Sydney about?"

I try not to stare at the hard points of her nipples under her dress. It's cold in here. There's a bite in the summer air outside tonight too after a day of rain and wind. Since Adley didn't bother with anything to cover her dress, I grabbed my suit jacket from behind the bar at the club and wrapped it around her shoulders before we left. She slid it off after her first messy bite of the burger so now I have the added accessory of a ketchup stain on the lapel.

"How's Sydney?" I reply, nudging my way past her question. I don't want to admit that I heard her talking about piercings.

"Good," she says around a small bite of a now soggy fry. "She has a new boyfriend."

I don't give two shits if she has twelve boyfriends. Sydney Tate is Adley's latest roommate. She's cute, ambitious and eager. I've met her twice and both times she was wearing nothing but lingerie. The first time might have been accidental as she was expecting another guy when she swung open the door

9

TROUBLEMAKER   *Deborah Bladon*

of their apartment. The second time was definitely calculated. The bra and panties she had on were sheer white. I saw everything. Not surprisingly, my cock slept through the whole damn thing.

I'm not into banging women who are that much younger than me. I'm just shy of thirty. Sydney's barely twenty-one. I won't hop on that train again. I like my women experienced, confident and not prone to misunderstanding that a good fuck is just that. It's a great time and not a promise of forever.

"Can I hang out at your place until he leaves?" She takes a sip of the chocolate shake through the straw, her eyes closing as she swallows.

I watch the motion of her neck. Christ, she's so fucking beautiful.

"You can stay all night if you want." I mean it. I have an extra bedroom. She's crashed there before. It's the reason why I stock the attached bathroom with the Matiz shower products she prefers. There's also a pair of sweats and a few white T-shirts in her size in the closet for her to sleep in.

She has a key to my place although she's never used it.

I have access to a key to her apartment because I own the building. It's a side project. Some men collect fine wine. I collect Manhattan real estate.

"I'll go home in a couple of hours." She dabs her mouth with a paper napkin. "Will you show me the mascara samples now? Then we can go to your place and work on that puzzle."

"That was tossed in the trash months ago," I say as I stand and reach for the back of her chair.

TROUBLEMAKER   *Deborah Bladon*

"You thought it went into the trash because I told you I'd take care of it." She wraps my suit jacket back around her body. "I hid it under the bed in the guest room."

"Why the fuck did you do that?" I catch her by the elbow as she stands.

"Simple." Her eyes lock on mine. "When you want something, you never give up. I knew one day you'd decide to take on the puzzle again and you'd beat it. Tonight might be the night."

"You have too much faith in me." I adjust the collar of my jacket, gently tugging her hair from beneath it, so the blonde waves tumble over the fabric. "Maybe I can't have everything I want in life, Ad."

The smile leaves her face. "I believe in you more than I believe in anyone else. You told me not to give up until I have everything I want. You need to follow your own advice."

I never want her to stop looking at me the way she is now. I won't lose what we have. Besides, this city is full of women ready and willing to get into bed with me. I can fuck Adley out of my system. Sooner or later that approach has to work.

If it doesn't, I'm screwed.

Chapter 3

Adley

I study the framed picture of Crew and his brother that's hanging on the wall near the kitchen in his apartment. I've walked past this spot countless times and yet, I've never noticed this particular image until tonight. It's no wonder. I'm always a tiny bit in awe when I come here. Crew's apartment is the quintessential bachelor pad, right down to the unobstructed view of New York City from the wall of windows that border this space and the dark furnishings that complement the expensive artwork.

My gaze skims over the photograph that looks like it was taken outside on a sunny day. They're standing next to one another, each with an arm over the other's shoulder. They're both striking to look at.

Kade, his younger brother, is attractive in a more subtle way than Crew. He's also completely different personality-wise. I should know. Crew set me up on a blind date with him last year.

"Hey." I turn to where Crew is sitting on his sofa. "Do you remember when you tried to get me to sleep with your brother?"

"Christ." He groans as he drops his head back onto the soft black leather. "Why the hell do you insist on reminding me about that? For the record, Kade is the one who asked me to set you two up as a favor to him."

I know that. Kade told me as much as soon as I arrived at the restaurant for our date. There was

TROUBLEMAKER   *Deborah Bladon*

undeniable instant chemistry between us, but it was a brother /sister vibe from the get-go. We still text each other a couple of times a month to check-in.

"At least we hit it off better than you did with Tilly."

"Matilda was something else, Ad." He laughs softly. "Don't get me wrong. She's a sweetheart, but she could have held back with her list of must-haves in a future husband until we left the restaurant. I didn't make it halfway through dinner before I called it a night."

When I set up my co-worker, Tilly, with Crew months ago, I didn't give it a lot of thought. I half-expected they'd sleep together. I've known Crew for close to two years and his type has always been the same. If she's tall with dark hair and a pretty face, she'll catch his eye.

He has a reputation for being a savage in bed. I wouldn't know from experience. We made a pact early on that we'd stay out of each other's reach in that regard. We're both too close to my best friend, Ellie, and her husband, Nolan, to screw up that match made in heaven.

If Crew and I crossed the line from friends to lovers, it wouldn't last. He's not interested in more than a night or two with the same woman and my sole focus right now is my career. Our friendship works for us and it's all we can ever be to each other. I know that even though sometimes my mind wanders into *what if* territory when I'm with him.

"She likes you a lot," I call from the kitchen as I grab a bottle of chilled water. "She still asks me if you're planning on taking her out for a second date."

TROUBLEMAKER   *Deborah Bladon*

"Tell her thanks, but no thanks." He appears at the breakfast bar that separates his custom kitchen from the rest of the open concept space.

We've always been transparent with each other, but not when it comes to intimacy. I don't go into details about the men I date and Crew keeps it to a minimum when he mentions the women he spends time with. It's part of our unspoken agreement to butt out of that aspect of each other's lives.

I asked him to stop looking for a man for me after my dinner with Kade. He requested the same regarding potential hookups the night of his date with Tilly. I want him to be happy, but I've learned that the only thing that keeps a smile on his face is keeping his libido sated. He does a good job of handling that on his own.

In fact, he has a woman waiting for him right now. I know that because I caught an unintentional glimpse of a text message that flashed on the screen of his phone back at the burger place. He got up to get the chocolate shake they forgot to give us when we picked up our food.

His phone vibrated on the table, my gaze dropped to it and I read the simple message.

I'm naked and waiting, love. I need you.

His eyes skimmed over the screen when he sat back down and he hasn't responded even though his phone repeatedly chimed when we were at the Matiz offices and again three times since we've gotten to his apartment.

"I can take off if you have plans." I wash down the words with some water. "You don't have to

TROUBLEMAKER   *Deborah Bladon*

entertain me. I'm sure Sydney's boyfriend has left by now."

"I don't have other plans." He sets his elbows on the counter and leans toward me. "My only plan is to hang out with one of my best friends."

I straighten. Crew doesn't know what his friendship means to me. Since Ellie and my other good friend, Brynn, have both found their happy-ever-afters, I've been on my own a lot more. It's not as though I need anyone to help me chart a path to a satisfying future. I don't.

I'm the first to admit that sometimes I'm lonely. Crew fills in that gap for me. We hang out like old friends and there's never a question about what I want out of my life. I'm bombarded with enough of that when I visit my folks.

I'm almost twenty-six-years-old. I have a stable job, a great place to live and good friends. I'm blessed as it is. Crew views his life the same way. It's one of the reasons we get along so well.

"What do you want to do?"

He narrows his eyes. "Not that fucking puzzle, Ad. I'll do anything but that."

"I can tell you about my list of must-haves in a future husband," I joke with a smirk. "My list is longer than Tilly's, so you better get …"

"There isn't a man on this earth who is good enough to be your husband," he interrupts me, his voice deep and smooth. His lips ease into a smile.

"Is that so?" I eye him suspiciously with a measured lift of my brows.

He turns to the left when the sound of my phone ringing cuts through the air. I stare at the

15

TROUBLEMAKER   *Deborah Bladon*

chiseled lines of his jaw and the shadow of whiskers that have settled there. He's incredible to look at. I can't deny that.

It's not a crime to think your best guy friend is insanely gorgeous.

"You're not on call, are you?" His brow perks as he turns back to look at me. "You don't drink when you're on call."

I don't. I can't. It's part of the employment contract I signed when I took the job with Dr. Hunt at his clinic. I'm on call every second weekend and at least one night during the week. "No. It's not work. I have no idea who it could be."

"Let's find out." He pushes against the counter and jogs across the room to where I dropped my purse on the table in the foyer. He scoops it up and delivers it to me. "Answer, Ad. People don't call after midnight unless it's serious."

He's right. Ellie's in bed by ten most nights because her kids are up at the crack of dawn. Brynn's schedule has changed too now that's she engaged and pregnant. Getting a call after midnight that isn't work-related is a rarity for me. When it does happen, it's almost always a booty call. I stopped answering those when I realized that I valued sleep more than the shitty feelings I was left with after a quick fuck with a man who didn't even bother to offer to pay my cab fare back home.

I dig my phone out of my clutch and glance down at the screen before I answer. "Hey, Syd. What's up?"

I'm greeted with a sob, then another. "Adley, I need you."

16

TROUBLEMAKER *Deborah Bladon*

"What's wrong?" I ask calmly because since Sydney moved in, I've become accustomed to her fragile heart and the consequences of that. She feels things deeply, loves fiercely and from what she told me about this latest guy, he's something special.

"I fought with Banner," she whimpers softly. "I need you to come home. Please, Ad. Come home."

I close my eyes. "Try to calm down. I'll leave right away. It won't take me more than twenty minutes to get there."

She whispers something inaudible before she ends the call.

"What's going on?" Crew's voice is even and gentle. "Has something happened to her?"

I tap my fingers lightly over the center of my chest. "I'd diagnose it as a broken heart. Treatment consists of time with her roommate, followed by a night with a new man."

"Is that how you mend your own heart?"

It's a loaded question and one I don't have the time, or inclination, to answer. "Maybe I've never had a broken heart."

He surveys my expression, but he'll find nothing of substance there. I've learned how to hide my emotions, not only from the people around me but myself too. "I'll take you home. We can grab a taxi."

I appreciate the offer. I've always relied on myself to get around the city. I know it like the back of my hand and I have no problem telling a taxi or Uber driver which route to take. I did it earlier when we left Crew's office to come here. The driver of the taxi Crew flagged down was going to go around Central Park. I told him to drive through it. It cut ten

TROUBLEMAKER   *Deborah Bladon*

minutes off our travel time. "You don't have to come with me. I'll get an Uber."

"I'm coming," he insists as he moves to pick up the suit jacket I was wearing earlier. "Wear this in the car. I'll walk you to your door and then I'll head back to the club for lock up."

I round the counter and let him drape the oversized garment around my shoulders. I want to ask him if he has a list of must-haves for a future wife but it hardly matters at this point. I'll nurse Sydney's bruised heart and he'll go to the club. He'll pick up a beautiful brunette there to bring back here or he'll respond to the text of the woman who is naked and waiting for him.

"You're such a gentleman," I say with a tilt of my head. "Do you treat all the women in your life this well?"

He reaches to tuck a strand of my hair behind my ear. His touch is soft as his fingertips linger on my cheek. "Only the ones who spill ketchup on my thousand dollar suit jacket."

"Oh shit." I swallow as I look down at the tailored black jacket. "I'll pay for dry cleaning. Can it be cleaned?"

"You'll pay for nothing." He leans down to brush his lips over my forehead. "I'm keeping the jacket as is. The stain is hardly noticeable and the jacket smells like you now."

I smile as I look into his eyes.

Flirtatious teasing has always been part of the dynamic of our friendship. This feels different. Maybe it's the rush from the drinks I had earlier. It

TROUBLEMAKER   *Deborah Bladon*

might be the look of dark intensity that's settled over his expression.

Whatever it is, I like it.

"Let's get you home." He slips effortlessly back into friendship mode with a tap on my shoulder. "Sydney needs you and I need another scotch before I call it a night."

I think I might need one too. That or a date with my battery operated boyfriend.

Chapter 4

Crew

My head aches with tension. That's what sleeping two hours and then getting up at the crack of dawn will do to me.

After I dropped Adley off at her apartment last night with a kiss to the back of her hand, I ran through the messages on my phone, laughing when I got to the thread from the woman I stood up so I could hang out with Ad. Messages that began with the promise of her naked and waiting ended with a charming *'Fuck You Asshole.'* Patience tends to be in short order when a woman is hungry for a skilled mouth and cock.

I deleted it all and I asked the taxi driver to take me to Veil East. I was prepared to go inside, grab another drink and find a woman to take home with me. I'm not a guy who sees the need to have a separate place for fucking. I do it in my bed, with the nightstand full of condoms next to me and my shower just a few feet away in the luxurious bathroom I recently had redesigned.

I don't care if a woman I screw knows where I live. I'm not an unknown in this town. I don't need to hide behind a wall of mystery. I'm young, unattached and I love sex. I should be able to enjoy it where I want. Preferably that's my apartment although I'm not opposed to a semi-public rendezvous. I've done it before and if the opportunity presented itself, I'd be all-in again.

TROUBLEMAKER   *Deborah Bladon*

Last night I didn't take anyone home and my pants stayed zipped.

I was adjusting my suit jacket after the driver pulled up to the club when my thumb ran over that damn ketchup stain. I lifted my forearm and inhaled, drowning in the scent of Adley's perfume. I didn't want another woman after that, so I told the driver to take me to the Matiz tower.

My night was spent going over the launch for our winter line. I got a jump on it and when I show the product lineup to Nolan tomorrow morning, he'll flip his shit.

If he weren't married with kids, I'd drag him down to the office now to go over it, but Sundays are reserved for his family. Often that includes Adley and me when dinner is about to be served. That's the reason I'm standing at the door to his apartment, dressed in jeans and a green polo with a bouquet of flowers for his wife in one hand and a kite for his kids in the other.

"Captain Crew," Ellie and Nolan's daughter, May, screams as she swings open the door. The nickname she blessed me with when she was a toddler has always stuck. "You're finally here."

It's the same reaction every time I see her. I cradled her in my arms when she was a day old. I love this kid like she's my own. Her brother, Jonas, holds an equal piece of my heart in his chubby little hands.

"I got you a kite." I hand it off to her as I close the door behind me. "You're going to share that with your brother. You can show him the ropes."

21

TROUBLEMAKER   *Deborah Bladon*

"I've never flown a kite before." She studies the package that contains everything a bright seven-year-old needs to assemble it. Her blonde ponytail bounces as she skips in place. "Are you going to take me to Central Park to fly it after we eat?"

"I'll take you and Jonas to the park. We can stop to pick up a bag of candy too. Don't tell your mom. She'll ruin everything."

"I'll ruin what?" Ellie, the redheaded firecracker Nolan married, comes into view. "What are you promising my daughter now?"

Fuck, I love that.

I know it's just a simple statement but I love hearing that. Ellie legally adopted May right after she and Nolan adopted Jonas. It was a technicality that she wanted in place since the woman who gave birth to May abandoned her. She's the best mom I've ever met and in five months, she's going to be a mother of three.

She's pregnant with a little boy. I'm holding out hope that he'll be named Crew but it's not looking good.

"Kite flying and candy." May wraps her arm around Ellie's waist. "You can come too, Mom."

"You're welcome to tag along if you can waddle fast enough to keep up with us." I hand the bouquet of daffodils to Ellie. "Ad can come too. She's the one who gave me the idea for the kite. She told me a couple of weeks ago that she was an expert kite pilot when she was a kid."

"I'm barely showing." Ellie lovingly runs her hand over her stomach. "Adley's not coming. It looks

TROUBLEMAKER   *Deborah Bladon*

like we'll have to figure out the kite flying on our own."

Work is the only reason Adley misses these things. I can't say the same for myself. I've bowed out more than a few times because of a random woman I couldn't tear myself away from.

Disappointment ripples through me. I've been looking forward to seeing her since I got out of bed. We ended last night on a different note than we normally do. She sat closer to me in the taxi, our legs brushing when the driver took a corner too sharply.

I've felt a new bond forming between us the past few months. It might be because we're sharing in the joy of Ellie and Nolan expanding their family, but it feels deeper than that to me.

"She's not on call." I sigh as I glance over Ellie's shoulder to where Nolan is sitting on the floor with his son in his lap, a toy train set in front of them. "Why would she stand us up?"

May lets out a laugh. "You don't know how to fly a kite, do you?"

I look down at her. "I can fly a kite better than Aunt Adley any day of the week."

"Go wash up for dinner." Ellie tugs playfully on May's ponytail. "I'm going to talk to Crew and we'll eat as soon as I'm done."

We both watch in silence as May takes off across the room with the kite package in her hand.

"What's going on with Ad?" I don't mince words. I know Ellie well enough to keep the bullshit to a minimum. "Is it her roommate?"

"Sydney?" Ellie says her name slowly. "What's happening with her?"

23

TROUBLEMAKER   *Deborah Bladon*

I wasn't looking for a question or two in reply to my question. I want an answer. "Her boyfriend did something last night that sent her into a tailspin. Adley had to go home to be the shoulder to cry on."

"Go home?" She waves an impatient hand at me. "You were with Ad last night? How was she?"

Three questions now instead of an answer. Fuck this is frustrating. "Why is Adley not coming to dinner, Bean?"

A brief smile passes over her lips at the nickname. Adley coined it years before I met either of them. Ellie is apparently her jelly bean, whatever the fuck that means. I took up the name myself because it used to irritate the shit out of Ellie. She's grown to love hearing me say it, even if she won't admit it.

"Your guess is as good as mine. She texted me an hour ago to tell me she wasn't coming. I sent her a message back asking why and she went silent."

I scrub a hand over my face. This is completely out of character for her. She's like a sister to Ellie. They tell each other everything. I should know. Nolan has let too many things slip about Adley that he was told in confidence by his wife. I'm the one who has benefited from that so I haven't told him to mind his own business yet.

"It's probably nothing." Ellie shrugs. "Maybe she has a date."

Trey Fucking Hale must have called her. Who the hell can blame him after the way she looked last night?

"Is there a baseball game tonight?" I gesture toward the television above the fireplace.

TROUBLEMAKER   *Deborah Bladon*

She shakes her head. "You know my rule about no television during dinner, Crew."

Sure. It detracts from our time together. It kills brain cells, and whatever else Ellie read online about how detrimental it is. I've heard it a thousand times.

"You're thinking what I'm thinking, aren't you?" she asks playfully.

I highly doubt that. I'm thinking about how good it would feel to have my hand wrapped around Hale's neck while I'm squeezing that signature cocky grin off his face.

My eyebrows draw together with the question we both know is sitting on the tip of my tongue.

"She gave Trey Hale her number last night." She smiles like that's the best thing that's happened since Nolan dropped to one knee and proposed. "I think they make the perfect couple, don't you?"

I think I should have gone with my first instinct and crushed his phone in my palm.

"She was so excited about it she sent me a text late last night. I hope she's with him right now." Ellie takes a step to the side. "She needs a guy like that. I need some food so let's eat."

I take the hint and walk toward the dining room even though I want to turn on my heel and go in search of Adley.

I can't. She gets to choose who she spends her time with. If that's Hale, so be it. I'm the one who has to learn to live with it.

Fuck if I know how to do that.

25

Chapter 5

Adley

If I had known that our dinner destination was Nova, I might have declined. It's recognized for not only the food but the fact that it's the place to come in Manhattan if you're in search of a surprise celebrity sighting.

That's the main reason there's a cluster of photographers across the street. They keep their cameras trained on the front of the restaurant and the endless line of chauffeured driven cars that drop off people who have made it their business to be famous.

I suspect that's why Trey brought me here. He hesitated when we exited the car. His hand was on my hip, his brown eyes focused on my face and not the front of my light blue dress. He put on a good show for anyone who was watching. I didn't take part since I wasn't handed a script on how to play the pro baseball star's date.

I'm winging it, including keeping my face covered by the large menu as Trey signs autographs and talks to his mostly female fans about the hamstring injury that has benched him for the past three weeks.

"Are you having fun, Adley?"

Thank God, he got my name right. When he called me earlier to ask me to dinner I thought I heard the distinctive sound of a 'sh' after the A. I'm used to it. My name is unusual enough to be confused with one that rolls off the tongue with familiarity.

TROUBLEMAKER   *Deborah Bladon*

There are a lot more Ashleys living in this city than Adleys.

I lower the menu enough to peek over it at him. "It's been a slice so far."

He smiles wolfishly. It's the same smile that has landed him countless sponsorship deals. His face is everywhere right now. He's riding the high and I'm the one by his side, even if it's just for tonight.

"I'll order us a bottle of wine."

I rest the menu on the table. "Are you a regular here?"

I'm genuinely interested. I did my research on him early this morning after I sent Ellie a text message to tell her that Trey asked for my number. She's picked up a fondness for baseball since she and Nolan have season tickets. It's not my scene although I have tagged along to a few games with her. Watching her cheering on the hometown team is the best part for me.

I had no idea that typing Trey Hale's name in a search engine would result in more than ten million hits. I spent less than an hour reading about his rise to fame and looking at pictures of him with some of the most well-known female faces on the planet.

He's not a stranger to Nova. This seems to be his go-to place when he wants the media to include him in the next news cycle.

Since he's not making headlines on the field right now, he's working another angle and I happen to have landed in the middle of that.

He runs a hand over his close-cropped brown hair. "Can I make a confession?"

TROUBLEMAKER   *Deborah Bladon*

If it has anything to do with the way he keeps stealing glances at my breasts, it's hardly a confession. It's obvious that he likes big tits. In at least half of the images of him online, his eyes are honed in on the chest area of his dates.

"Confess your sins. I won't tell." I smile at him.

The hint of amusement in my voice relaxes him. I see it in his shoulders and the way his jaw stops ticking. "I don't know where else to go. Whenever I ask a woman out, she'll say she wants to go to Nova. I didn't ask you because, well, I thought you'd say the same thing."

I take a sip of the water that the server brought us after we were seated. "Where else do you like to eat?"

"Other than here, I only ever go to this pizza place in Times Square."

I watch him as he watches the people around us. He's hesitant, ducking his face down when someone looks in our direction. Maybe I misread him. Maybe he's not the famewhore I thought he was.

"If you could eat anything right now, what would it be?"

Shit. I stepped right into that one.

His tongue darts out to wet his lips. "If I said you that would be out of line, wouldn't it?"

"I don't…not on the first date."

"It's technically our second since I bought you a drink last night."

"I get free drinks at Veil East so technically you didn't buy me a drink."

TROUBLEMAKER   *Deborah Bladon*

He muddles that over with a glance around the room. "I got the feeling last night that you would have come home with me if I would have asked. I mean, before Benton showed up."

Looking back on that now, I'm glad Crew came to talk to me when he did. I'd had one or two too many free drinks. I was enjoying the moment and Trey's attention. I probably would have gone home with him and left his place with a hangover and at least a year's worth of regret.

"I try not to focus on the past. We're here now."

"So, this is our first date?" His eyes sparkle when he smiles. "We've established that you're not coming home with me tonight. I'm free tomorrow for our second date."

"I'm busy unless you understand that I won't be sleeping with you until I'm ready."

He laughs. His entire demeanor has changed since we arrived at Nova. He's more laid back now. "Understood. I like you, Adley."

I like him too. He seems like a nice enough guy.

"Let's get back to my original question." I fold my hands together on the table. "If you could eat anything…any type of food right now, what would it be?"

He grins broadly at my subtle correction. Then he leans his forearms on the table, his voice lowering to a hushed whisper. "I'm supposed to steer clear of greasy shit, but I've been craving a juicy burger and fries. Do you know where we could get that?"

"Do I ever," I say as I push back my chair. "Follow me, Trey. You're going to think you died and went to burger heaven."

Chapter 6

Crew

If you're worth a million bucks, there's no reason in hell why you shouldn't look like a million bucks. Take me for instance. I'm not dressed to the nines tonight. After I left Nolan and Ellie's apartment, I swung by my place and changed into a thin white sweater. I tugged that on, slipped on some black shoes and I look like a million and a quarter, even though I'm wearing jeans.

Trey Hale, on the other hand, looks like three dollars. He's wearing the same sorry ass suit he was wearing last night, but tonight he's got a smile on his face that could light up the holiday tree in Rockefeller Center.

If I didn't want to wring his neck, I might be inclined to send him to my tailor to get fitted for at least one custom suit. He needs it. He's the face of the most celebrated baseball team in the country and yet, he looks like he slept in the dumpster around the corner.

His smile brightens when the familiar blonde next to him touches his knee.

Adley is obviously interested in what's hidden inside his wrinkled pants. He's got his eyes pinned on her tits.

Lucky me that I get to witness this.

"Your bodyguard just walked in," Hale announces after he manages to unglue his eyes from the front of the tight blue dress she's wearing so he can glance in my direction.

Adley cranes her neck to look at where I'm standing in the entrance of the burger restaurant she brought me to last night. Apparently, I'm not as special as I thought I was.

"What are you doing here?" The corners of her mouth curve up in a smile as I approach. "Didn't you have dinner with Nolan and Bean?"

"Bean?" Hale has the same reaction I did the first time I heard Ad say Ellie's nickname. "Who is that?"

"Our friend," I say without hesitation. "We missed you tonight, Ad."

Her gaze falls to the floor. "Trey invited me to dinner...dinner at Nova."

"Yet, you're here." I survey the almost vacant restaurant. "Did Nova run short of food?"

"Adley suggested this place instead." Trey reaches to grab her hand. "I'm glad she did. The burgers are the best I've ever had."

Her face brightens with the compliment. He's either oblivious to what a real burger should taste like or he's under Adley's spell. I can't blame him. She's gorgeous tonight. Her hair is pinned up. She's wearing a dress I've never seen her in before. She looks like ten million dollars.

"I'm glad we agree on that." She drops Hale's hand and turns toward me in her chair, giving me my first full view of her.

Jesus. I feel that familiar sizzle race down my spine. The desire for her is instant and intense.

TROUBLEMAKER   *Deborah Bladon*

"Are you hungry?" she goes on, "I always knew you had a huge appetite, but I had no idea you could eat twice in one night."

I could eat you twice in one night and the craving wouldn't be any less than it is right now.

Hale smirks as if he knows exactly where my thoughts wandered off to. I'm not fucking surprised. He's thought about going down on her. I'd bet my last dollar that he's fantasized about everything he wants to do with her.

"You picking up some take-out, Benton?" He trails his fingers along Adley's back.

My skin crawls at the sight of his hand on her. I have to take a step back before I pull him from the chair and toss him out the door.

"I was actually grabbing some food for Ad," I say it to her, ignoring the fact that his fingers are now circling a path over her exposed shoulder. "I thought she might not be feeling well after last night. I'm glad she recovered."

"She feels great to me." He squeezes her arm and she flinches. "We're going to finish up here and then head out. It was good to see you."

Fuck you too, Hale.

Adley springs to her feet, leaving Hale's hand hanging in mid-air. "You were getting me food because you thought I was hungover?"

"You told me once that the quickest way to cure it is to eat your favorite food," I say it, knowing that she'll remember when she first said those words to me. She was in my bed, fully clothed and on top of the blankets when I was nursing a hangover courtesy of New Year's Eve. She cooked for me. It tasted

33

TROUBLEMAKER   *Deborah Bladon*

horrible but I didn't give a shit. I spent the day sleeping in my tuxedo shirt and pants because I was too sick to change. She was there for hours, by my side, making certain that I had everything I needed.

"It's true." She nods to exaggerate the point. "I already ate, but I'm touched that you thought of me."

I never stop.

Coming here for take-out was part of my longshot plan to see her tonight. I sent her a text message when I was in Central Park with Nolan's family. By the time I'd made it back to my place over an hour later, there was still no response.

I decided to make a house call with her favorite burger in hand even though I knew there was a good chance she was on a date. I didn't know that I'd run into her here with Hale drooling all over her.

"I'm going to take off." I hold Adley's gaze. "It was good to see you."

She leans back slightly and looks me over. "Are you all right? Is everything okay?"

I catch both her hands in mine and bring them to my lips. "I was concerned when you didn't make it to dinner at Ellie's. I'm glad you're good, Ad."

Her eyes lock on mine. "You're the best friend I've ever had."

I kiss her knuckles once more before I drop her hands. "I'm always around if you need me."

Her full lips part as if she's going to say something, but there's nothing.

"Enjoy your night, Crew." Hale darts to his feet, his arm wrapping around her waist. "I know we will."

She doesn't acknowledge him at all. Her gaze

34

TROUBLEMAKER   *Deborah Bladon*

stays focused on my face. I turn and walk away, wishing like hell I was the one taking her home with me.

Chapter 7

Adley

"You're blowing up all over social media right now, Ad," Tilly whispers to me as she readies the paperwork for the slew of patients waiting to see Dr. Hunt and the veterinarian he brought on board two months ago, Dr. Carolyn Gallo. Business is brisk.

I look at Tilly. I know exactly what she's talking about. Ellie sent me a one-line text message last night.

You're officially a #halesbabe.

Whenever a picture of Trey and a woman is posted online by either a Hale fan or the paparazzi, it's tagged with the hashtag halesbabe. Last night I joined that club when an image of Trey and I that was taken outside Nova was posted to an Instagram account. The picture went viral within hours.

As of this morning, it's been shared more than ten thousand times and it has ten times as many likes.

Those stats don't impress me. I don't want or need that kind of attention.

"What's he like?" Tilly pretends to busy herself with the file in front of her. "Tell me everything."

I hate talking about personal things at work. I take this job seriously. Dr. Hunt took a chance on me when he gave me this position after I graduated with a Bachelor of Science degree and a love of animals. I've worked hard for him ever since.

TROUBLEMAKER   *Deborah Bladon*

"We had a burger, talked about our careers, and then he took me home." I don't look at her. I have too much to do today to waste time going over my uneventful date.

After Crew left the burger place, I told Trey that I needed to get home. He called for his chauffeured car and once we arrived at my apartment, I said goodnight without a kiss.

"There has to be more to it than that, Adley." Tilly sighs and taps her toe on the tile floor. "You don't have dinner with the most famous pitcher in the league and go home after dinner."

"You do if you're me."

Her eyes dart to the waiting room. We're booked full for the entire day. Neither of us has time to stand around talking about Trey. "Give me one juicy detail and I swear I'll leave you alone."

I pick up the file for Brazen, the small terrier, who is here for his yearly check-up. "Trey's left nipple is pierced."

"What the hell?" She doesn't even try to keep that to an acceptable level. Every single person in the waiting room turns toward us.

"Shh," I hush her. "You're going to get us both fired."

"You saw his nipple piercing?"

I shake my head as I tuck a requisition into the file of a labradoodle set to walk through the door any second with its owner. "I met him at Veil East on Saturday night. He told me about it when we were dancing."

"That's hot."

37

TROUBLEMAKER   *Deborah Bladon*

"What's hot?" Dr. Hunt's unmistakable deep voice startles us both as he exits his office next to the reception desk.

I turn when Tilly answers him. "Beacon's temperature, Dr. The cat in exam room two is burning up. I'm ready if you are."

Skepticism knits his brow. "I'm ready, Matilda. Follow me."

She does, with her tongue hanging out of her mouth and her brows wiggling. Dr. Hunt is a handsome man. He knows it. Every person in the waiting room does too which is why all heads turn as he walks past with Tilly hot on his heel.

***

"It's been days since you two had dinner. Are you going to see him again this week?" Ellie chews on the end of a carrot. "If you are, I think you should wear that strapless red dress you wore to my birthday party. It shows off all your assets."

"Like my ass?" I squirm on the chair I'm sitting on next to her dining table. I came here to decompress after three very long days of work. I've stayed late each night since my date with Trey. Two of my co-workers are out sick so that means extra overtime for everyone who hasn't caught the flu bug yet.

"That and other things." She circles her hand in front of her chest.

"My breasts aren't that big." I look down at the front of my scrubs. It's my go-to outfit for work since Dr. Hunt requires that every one of his employees

38

TROUBLEMAKER   *Deborah Bladon*

wears the personalized blue scrubs he supplies. They have our names stamped above a small pocket on the left chest area. On the right side is the name of the clinic, Premier Pet Care. "I'm a C-Cup."

"I'm going to be a C-cup in a few months." She juts out her chest. "My boobs have already gotten bigger. Nolan is a fan."

"Don't tell me about what Nolan digs behind closed doors, Bean." I place my index finger over my lips to shush her.

"Fine." She huffs as she takes another small bite of her snack. "Let's talk about when you're going to see Trey again."

If he had his way it would be tonight. He sent me a dozen roses at work today. By the time I had a break and was able to text him to thank him, the flowers weren't my secret anymore. Tilly posted a picture of them with the halesbabe hashtag. She tagged me in it, so now my name is out there as the woman Trey is currently seeing.

"I don't know," I confess on a sigh. I'm in no hurry to go out with him again. That's why I told him I was busy tonight. My plans consist of this visit with Ellie before I head home to take a nice long bath. If I were into him, I would have taken him up on his offer straightaway.

"Why the hesitation to see him again?" Ellie puts the rest of the carrot on a napkin. "He's good-looking, successful, and he sent you flowers."

"How do you know that?"

She picks her phone up from the table and opens Instagram. The picture Tilly took of the roses

39

TROUBLEMAKER   *Deborah Bladon*

pops into view. "That right there is the sign of a guy who is eager."

Eager to fuck. The feeling is not mutual.

"I haven't even kissed him yet, Bean."

"You can correct that by asking him out for dinner."

"I accept." Crew steps into view around the corner from the hallway. "Where are you taking me?"

"Where is my husband?" Ellie pushes herself to her feet. "I told him to pick up some groceries on his way home. Did he?"

"He got everything on that long ass list you texted him." Crew wraps his arm around Ellie's shoulder. "Your pregnancy cravings are disgusting, by the way. Keep in mind, that I don't say that lightly. My sister ate olives with peaches before she popped her kid out."

"That sounds delicious." Ellie licks her bottom lip. "We have olives. I need some peaches."

"You need to go find your husband." Crew jerks a thumb toward the kitchen. "He's half-way through a package of coconut cookies. Unless you stop him at the pass, you're not getting any of those tonight."

Ellie takes off at a quick walk.

"Did you come here straight from work?" Crew settles into the chair Ellie was just in. "Or are you trying to drive the male population of Manhattan crazy with that outfit."

"I look good in this."

"You look good in anything, Ad."

I feel a blush creep over my cheeks. He looks good in anything too, especially the navy blue three-

TROUBLEMAKER   *Deborah Bladon*

piece suit he's wearing. "I did come straight from work. I wanted to see the kids, but they're having dinner with Nolan's folks."

He looks around the dining room. "I don't see a dozen red roses anywhere. Your purse must be huge."

I'm taken aback by his admission. I know he follows the Premier Pet Care social media feeds. I didn't realize he followed them that closely. "You're talking about the roses Trey sent me."

"I sure am, Hale's Babe."

There's a hint of sarcasm in his tone or is it jealousy?

It can't be that. He reminds me often enough that I'm his best friend.

"I left them at work." I shrug. "That way I can fall in love with them all over again tomorrow morning."

His finger taps the edge of the wooden table. "Be careful, Ad. He tried to pick up my friend, Sophia, in the club right after it opened. He's a player, in more ways than one."

"What's that old saying about the pot calling the kettle black?"

A provocative smile covers his mouth. "You're on fire tonight, HB."

HB. Hale's babe.

Crew has to know how much I hate that.

"You're both welcome to stay for dinner." Ellie walks back into the dining room with a coconut cookie in her hand. "I'm making a veggie spaghetti dish. You'll love it."

TROUBLEMAKER   *Deborah Bladon*

"'I'll pass." Crew pushes up from the table. "I need to pack."

"Where are you going?" Ellie gets the question out before I have a chance.

"I'm heading west in the morning." He eyes me. "Back to the place it all began for the four of us."

"Vegas?" I lift a brow. "Why are you going to Vegas?"

I know he has a club there, Veil West, and there's a Matiz store there too. He has business there. I had no reason to ask him why the sudden trip to Vegas, but I want to know.

"I'm going to check in on a few things." He nudges Ellie with his shoulder. "Maybe look for a gift for a certain mom-to-be, and I'll take a day or two to hang with an old friend."

I don't bother asking who because I can guess within three tries. It's the woman he met the same night Ellie met Nolan. Lucia Turin, the co-owner of this club there. He bought controlling interest from her and re-branded the place with great success.

A few months after the deal closed, I overheard him telling Nolan on the phone how he had christened the club with Lucia. They'd fucked in one of the private rooms of the club on the night of the re-opening.

I scratch the back of my neck, suddenly feeling the need for a long soak in my tub.

"You deserve it." Ellie pats his chest. "Nolan says you've been hauling ass at Matiz lately and I know the club sucks up a lot of your time."

TROUBLEMAKER   *Deborah Bladon*

"I need the break." His eyes drift over my face. "I feel like I'm suffocating in New York. A week in Vegas will give me the perspective I need."

It's cryptic. I can't tell if it's directed at me or not.

"Take care of this one, Ad." He kisses the top of Ellie's head. "That's my godson she's hauling around."

Mine too.

"I always do," I say softly. "Take care of yourself."

"That's the plan." He holds my gaze for a beat before he leaves the room to talk to Nolan.

I've never missed him when he's left on any of the countless trips he's taken before. I can still hear his voice in the kitchen, so why does it feel like he's already a million miles away?

Chapter 8

Crew

There are three things I can count on when I'm in Las Vegas. I'll win at the poker table. I owe that to my mom and two brothers. We spent every Saturday night when I was a kid around our kitchen table playing Texas Hold'em for a pot of nickels and dimes.

I have no doubt when I'm here that I'll eat well. That's because I own a stake in one of the best restaurants in Nevada. It's located in the most exclusive resort on the strip. I'm a silent partner, but when I sit down to indulge in a delicious dinner, I'm anything but quiet. I love a good meal, and I let the server, the chef and anyone within earshot know it.

The last sure thing is a good time with Lucia Turin. An exotic, brown-haired beauty with a mind for business; she's a constant during my visits to Sin City. I met her two years ago when she was standing outside her club.

We talked, had a drink and an hour-and-a-half later, I was between her legs, balls deep inside of her and ready to negotiate a deal that would give me controlling interest in that club.

She held out on the club, not the sex. She never holds out on the sex.

That is as true tonight as it was the first time I laid eyes on her. It was the same night I met Adley, but she blurred into the background back then. She stood on the sidelines as I hammered out a deal with Ellie outside the club. I wanted her to move to New

TROUBLEMAKER *Deborah Bladon*

York to take on the job as head security officer at our flagship store on Fifth Avenue. She was working as a casino security guard at the time, and I watched her take down a man twice her size with ease. I knew I needed Ellie on the Matiz team. I had no idea back then that she'd end up marrying Nolan.

Ad stood in the shadows that night, watching me negotiating with her best friend. I caught her eye once, but I was oblivious to what was right in front of me. I wanted the same thing I always did and that was a tall woman with a mane of dark hair and a thin frame.

"You're still dressed." Lucia enters the main living area of the massive hotel suite I call home when I'm here. I can see her reflection in the floor-to-ceiling windows now that night has settled over the city and the lights of the strip guide the way to a multitude of sins.

I don't need to leave my suite for that. Lucia is already naked.

We'd shared a meal in my restaurant and then two hours in our club. It felt familiar, comfortable and when she suggested we come up to my suite, I didn't see a reason not to.

I do now.

While she was freshening in the washroom, I sent Adley a text message.

I've been here for four days and I've held out reaching out until now. I needed room to breathe and clear my head.

I couldn't shake the vision of Hale's hand on her bare shoulder at the burger place. Eventually, that

45

morphed into mental images of the two of them in his bed.

I couldn't be close when that happens. I had to bolt. I thought if I got out of the city I could handle the envy. I was dead wrong. I doubt like hell that a trip to the moon would ease what keeps rolling through my gut. Jealousy is a miserable beast, especially when you envy a man who has something that's been within your reach for years.

I pull my gaze from Lucia's nude body to look down at my phone again.

I miss you.

Those were the three words in the text message I sent to Adley in haste.

I miss you too.

Those were the four words she sent back that felt like I'd been given a gift.

They don't hold the promise of anything. They're simple words between two close friends, but I've been craving them for days, even if I didn't realize it until now.

"I've been dying to suck your cock since dinner." Lucia approaches, her hands trailing over her tits. "Take off your trousers, Crew."

It's an offer I shouldn't be able to refuse. Lucia knows what I like. She'll drop to her knees right here and blow me. She'll crawl into my bed and we'll spend the rest of my time in Vegas the way we always do when we're together. Little sleep, countless condoms, and an understanding that when I head back to New York, she's as free to do whoever the hell she wants as I am.

TROUBLEMAKER   *Deborah Bladon*

"Not tonight." I shake off her hand as she reaches for the front of my gray pants. "Get dressed."

"Not tonight?" she parrots back with a sneer." Exactly what does that mean?"

I turn to look at her, keeping my eyes focused on her face because what's below her neck doesn't interest me anymore. "It means I don't want to fuck you, Lucia. I want you to leave."

"Slow down, lover." Her hands move to caress my biceps through the white button down shirt I'm wearing. "You held me at bay for four days and now that I'm here, you're telling me to fuck off?"

I have kept her at arm's length since I landed earlier this week. I had work to do and I know from experience, that once Lucia gets her claws in me, business takes a back seat.

I promised her that we'd spend the next three days together.

"I'm not telling you to fuck off." I reach for my suit jacket. I'd tossed it onto the back of the plush sofa when we arrived. "Put this on."

"Why?" She pushes it away with both hands. "You suddenly don't like my body? I've never heard a complaint from you before."

She's right. I've only ever offered compliments. She's a beautiful woman who is skilled in the sack. Her business acumen makes her the perfect fit for me, yet we've never taken things between us beyond our shared interest in Veil West and a satisfying fuck whenever I'm in town.

"You won't hear one now." I turn back to the window and the lights that promise an experience unlike any other. Vegas comes with a rich treasure of

47

TROUBLEMAKER   *Deborah Bladon*

hope mixed with every wicked pleasure imaginable. That's the reason it's one of my favorite places on this earth. "It's not about you."

She parts her feet and plants her hands on her hips. "You need to fuck, Crew. Whatever is on your mind will cease to exist once your cock hits the back of my throat."

My dick doesn't even twitch with those words. "I'm not in the mood."

"You're always in the mood." She cocks her head to the side.

"Not tonight." I bark back to her reflection. Her hand darts between her thighs. The temptation bait she's casting in my direction is a waste of her time.

She throws her head back and moans. I look down at my phone again. I want to call Adley. I want to ask how her week has been. I want to tell her that I've been thinking about her constantly, but I can't. Nothing has changed between us since I left. We're still *just friends* and she's still hanging out with Hale judging by an image that was posted to a random woman's Instagram account six hours ago and tagged with the halesbabe hashtag.

It was a picture of Ad and Hale at a café. The fingers of her left hand were touching the front of her neck. It's a sure sign that she was uncomfortable in the moment. Hale's not the guy for her even if twenty-thousand people liked the picture and more than five hundred commented on what a perfect couple they are.

Idiots. They don't know her.

TROUBLEMAKER   *Deborah Bladon*

"I'm going to come," Lucia cries from where she's still standing, her hand moving in a frantic pace to get herself off.

I turn and walk past her, leaving her alone to enjoy the climax she needs, and I want no part of.

Chapter 9

Adley

"Crew will be back in three days," Ellie tells May as we stand at the corner of Broadway and Eighty-First. "You can explain to him what happened to the kite then."

May shields her eyes from the bright mid-day sun with her hand as she looks up at her mom. "Why can't we just call him? He told me that if I need him that I should call."

He's told me the same thing countless times. I was tempted to reach out to him yesterday, but visions of him in bed with Lucia kept me from making the call. He did send me a text message shortly after two this morning when I was up getting a glass of water. It said that he missed me.

I sent him a response almost immediately telling him that I missed him too, and then I waited for more. Nothing came and now it's almost twelve hours later and I haven't heard another word from him. I won't until he's back in Manhattan.

"What happened to the kite?" I step onto the street once the light changes. "Did you get it caught in a tree?"

"No." May reaches forward to grab my hand. "I gave it to a friend."

I squeeze her hand in mine. She's so much like Ellie that it's hard to believe that they're not related by blood. Ellie was homeless when we met and yet she would have given the few possessions she did have to

TROUBLEMAKER   *Deborah Bladon*

anyone who needed them. Her good heart has rubbed off on her daughter.

May and I skip up onto the curb once we've crossed the street. Ellie does the same with Jonas by her side.

"Your friend didn't have a kite?" I look down at May. She's wearing a pair of blue shorts and a blue T-shirt. Our outfits are almost identical right down to our flat-heeled sandals. Mine are nude, hers a sparkly pink.

"He doesn't have many toys." She pushes a pebble on the sidewalk with her foot. "Mom took me to fly the kite yesterday and he was there with his little brother. I gave them the kite because I knew Captain Crew would have done the same thing."

She's right.

"He's going to be proud of you." I start walking up Broadway holding tight to her hand with Ellie and Jonas trailing behind us. "You did the right thing by thinking of your friend first."

"That's what I thought too." She looks up at me, her brown eyes widening. "Captain says you and dad are his best friends. Your best friend is a boy and mine is too."

"Your best friend is the boy you gave the kite to?"

"Zane," she says as her cheeks blush. "He's cute."

"I bet he thinks the same thing about you." I squeeze her hand again as we walk toward her favorite bistro for lunch. "He sounds like a pretty special best friend to me. It was kind of you to give that kite to Zane. Crew will think so too."

51

TROUBLEMAKER   *Deborah Bladon*

"I can't wait until he gets back from his trip." She skips faster and I up my pace to keep up with her. "I hope he's not having so much fun that he stays there forever."

He might. Lucia is perfect for him. It's only a matter of time before he realizes that.

***

"Is that blood on your shirt?" Sydney leans in to get a closer look. "That is blood, Adley. Do you know how unsanitary that is?"

"I had to draw blood from a Dalmatian today. Obviously he wasn't cooperative."

I should have known it wouldn't be an easy shift when I was called in on my day off. I'd just finished sharing an ice cream covered dessert brownie with May when Tilly called to ask me to cover the rest of her shift because she felt sick. I couldn't decline. She's done the same for me on more than one occasion.

"You have to change out of your scrubs before the party starts." Sydney runs her hands over her short white dress. "I'm wearing this but you can wear anything but what you have on right now."

A party? Seriously?

I have to work again tomorrow. I can't party until I drop tonight. I'm close to dropping now I'm so exhausted.

"You're having a party? How many people are coming?"

52

TROUBLEMAKER   *Deborah Bladon*

"It's more a pizza and beer hangout to watch the game." She bites her bottom lip. "How many would be too many?"

One. That's what I want to say, but I don't.

I was looking forward to taking a bath tonight and then watching a movie. Obviously, that's not happening now.

"How many, Syd?" I rest my hip against the counter.

"Twenty," she replies quickly. "Two."

I take a deep breath and then let it out; using the minute it affords me to calm down enough that I don't offend her. "You know that sometimes I work odd hours. It would help me a lot, in the future, if we talked about having that many people over before the invites were sent out."

Her bottom lip trembles slightly. "I messed up, didn't I? I'm sorry, Ad. I thought we could both use some fun. I've seen how hard you've been working lately."

I'm not angry. It's hard to be mad at someone who bounced into my life and has become such a good friend in a short period of time. "Normally, I'd be all over the idea of a party but I'm wiped tonight."

"I can cancel it." She reaches forward to grab her phone from the counter. As she slides it toward her, she knocks my keys to the hardwood floor. "Shit. I'm going to get my ass thrown out of here before the night is over."

I bend down to pick up my keys, jingling them in my hand. My eyes catch on the key that I've never used. It opens the door to Crew's apartment.

53

TROUBLEMAKER   *Deborah Bladon*

When he handed it to me he told me that the doormen had a standing order to let me in the building if I ever showed up. He also made it crystal clear that if I ever needed a place to crash, I should consider myself welcome in his guest room.

I stayed the night there twice before. Once when my power was out because of a breaker issue and the second time was when the city came to a standstill because of a snowstorm. I didn't want to deal with the hassle of trying to find a ride back to my place, so I slept in the plush bed reserved for guests. Both nights, I slept like a baby.

"I don't want you to cancel and you're not getting thrown out." I smile. "I love having you as a roommate."

"So you'll change and get ready for the party? Trey Hale's not in the line-up tonight. Do you think he'd want to come over? My friends would freak."

Trey would love to but he's sitting in the dugout tonight watching his teammates take on the team ranked second in their division. He called me right before I left work today. I didn't answer so he left a message asking me if I wanted to watch the game from the team owner's skybox. I texted him on my way home telling him that I had to take a rain check.

Our relationship hasn't progressed beyond meeting for dinner or coffee yet. He did kiss me goodbye after we met at a café yesterday, but there wasn't even a spark. It was a close-mouthed, uninspired meeting of lips and nothing more.

"Trey's at the game tonight." I dip my chin down. "I think I'm going to take off. You can have the

TROUBLEMAKER   *Deborah Bladon*

place all to yourself. I won't be back until tomorrow after my shift."

"Someone has a hot date with a smoking hot baseball player after the game."

"That someone isn't me," I say simply. "I'm going to go hang out at a friend's place."

Her gaze narrows. "Why do I feel like I'm chasing you out of your own home?"

"You're not." I shake my head to reinforce the point. "I want you to have a good time with your friends. This is as much your home as it is mine."

"Does that mean we can use your bedroom for any extracurricular activities?" Her eyebrows dance. "I mean I only have that one queen size bed in my room."

"I'm locking my bedroom door before I leave." I smile as I jingle my keys in my hand.

"I was totally joking," she says, nudging my shoulder. "It's mostly friends from high school coming over. Friends who are girls."

I laugh. "I'm still locking my bedroom door."

"Thanks for letting us hang out here. You're the best." She leans forward to hug me. "I hope your night will be as good as mine."

Chapter 10

Crew

I spent my day in a meeting with the manager of the Matiz store in Vegas followed by five hours on a plane that had run dry of whiskey, beer and anything harder than a non-alcoholic white wine. The only redeeming part of that flight was the man sitting next to me. He owns a shopping complex in Boston. I've been scouting the city looking for a space for our newest Matiz boutique.

I'll fly there next week and buy him lunch. Fate does shine her bright light on me occasionally.

"I'll have someone bring your bags up, sir." The driver I occasionally use smiles as he opens the car door so I can exit. "It won't be more than ten minutes."

It better not be. I want a hot shower and a scotch. I'll have to squeeze a shave in there somewhere. My five o'clock shadow has grown into a light beard over the past few days.

I made the decision to come back to Manhattan as soon as Lucia stomped out of my suite with an impressive trail of curse words falling from her lips. I called the airline myself, since rousing my assistant from bed at three in the morning would earn me a shitty attitude from her once I showed back up in the office. I didn't see the need to wake the woman up in the middle of the night to handle a call I'm perfectly capable of taking on myself.

TROUBLEMAKER   *Deborah Bladon*

I should have risked the blowback and called Nancy.

The airline booked me on a connecting flight through Atlanta first thing in the morning. I was packed, ready and eager to board when the flight was cancelled.

Shit happens so I got the gate agent to rebook me on a flight an hour later. It had two connections and an empty seat in coach so I was on board, until I wasn't.

I was bumped onto the standby list for the next flight and by then, Nancy was at her desk in New York. I called her. She took care of it and got me on a direct in the afternoon. That gave me time to revisit the manager of the Matiz store in Vegas to talk about the launch of the fall line of products that will hit stores before summer is half over.

For a day that started out in hell, it's ending in heaven.

I'm home.

I reach in my pocket and pull out a hundred to tip the driver. I'm not an overly generous guy but he's one of the good ones. He kept quiet so I could close my eyes on the drive from LaGuardia.

"Thank you, sir." He bows when I hand him the bill.

I catch him by his shoulder. "I'm not a fucking prince, Bill. Don't hurt your back for a hundred. You need to drop the sir shit too or your next tip is a dollar. It's Crew, not sir. I told you that last time."

"Yes, Crew." He pockets the cash. "I'll get those bags sent right up. Enjoy your night, sir."

TROUBLEMAKER   *Deborah Bladon*

I huff out a laugh as I turn to walk into the building. "A dollar, Bill. One fucking dollar next time."

***

Jesus.

Fate isn't just shining her bright light on me tonight, she's handing me every dream I've ever had and then some.

I'm in my apartment. It's dark, the only light illuminating the main room is the flicker from the television.

I knew something was up as soon as I opened the door, walked into the foyer and heard voices. It didn't take but a beat for me to realize it was the television. It wouldn't have been the first time I've come home to find it on. The woman who stops by twice a week to tidy up the place is notorious for leaving it blaring once she's done her work and left.

Tonight is different.

I stalked across the room to turn it off, but I stopped in place when I noticed an open laptop, a smartphone, a half-eaten bowl of microwave popcorn and an empty soda can on my coffee table. I stock that brand of soda in my fridge for just one person.

I looked toward the guest room but the door was wide open and the lights were off. That's when I rounded the leather couch and came close to dropping to my knees.

Adley York is fast asleep on my couch.

I can't help but stare. My cock can't help but swell.

TROUBLEMAKER *Deborah Bladon*

Her blonde hair is splayed out on the pillow beneath her head. Her lips are parted slightly and her body is more than I ever could have imagined.

One arm is bent above her head. The other is resting on her stomach; her bare stomach.

Beautiful Adley is nude from the waist up. Her breasts are round and full with nipples I'm dying to suck into pebbled peaks.

The only thing covering her body is a small pair of sheer white panties that provide just a tease of a smooth pink cunt underneath them.

She looks like a sinful angel.

I run my hand over the front of my black pants. I'm hard as stone. My erection is pulsing with need.

The dirty part of me wants to fist it, waking her with a grunt and a pinch of her nipple before I shoot my hot release all over that flawless skin.

I shake my head. *What the fuck am I doing?*

I back away, my eyes never leaving her body. This may very well be the only chance I get to see this in my lifetime and I want to implant it in my mind so later tonight when I'm in the shower, or a year or ten from now, I can jerk off to the memory of the sight of her tits and pussy.

Fuck, I want a taste of that.

My breathing labors as I quietly move back to the foyer. I can't let the doorman pound on the door the way he usually does when he brings up my bags. It may startle her enough that she'll wake and then she'll be horrified that I saw her wearing nothing but a pair of panties that I wish I could have so I can smell her scent whenever I want.

59

TROUBLEMAKER   *Deborah Bladon*

For fuck's sake. I need to get a grip.

I pick up my briefcase and exit the apartment with a soft click of the door.

I know she's a heavy sleeper. I saw it the night she slept over during a snow storm. I had to practically kick in the guest room door to get her out of bed to have breakfast with me.

I hear the ding of the service elevator in the distance which means the doorman is about to drop a suitcase and a wardrobe bag at my feet.

I fish my phone from the inner pocket of my suit jacket. I pull up Adley's contact information and hit the call button. The annoying song she has pinned as her ringtone when she's on call starts up behind the closed door. It's loud as hell and for good reason. It's the only thing that will get her out of bed and to the clinic.

It continues unanswered until it goes to voicemail.

Shit.

I set out down the corridor at a quick pace passing the semi-private elevator I just exited before I round the corner as the service elevator's doors shut behind the doorman.

I call her again, hoping that the incessant music will jar her awake. By some miracle she answers on the third ring, her voice soft and groggy. "Yes. Hi."

I stalk toward the elevator and the stunned doorman. I don't want Adley to know how close I am. I want to give her at least a two minute warning before I open the apartment door again. "Ad, it's me. What are you up to tonight?"

TROUBLEMAKER   *Deborah Bladon*

The doorman shoots me a puzzled look. I half-shrug as I drop my briefcase and lean a hand on his shoulder to catch my breath.

"Crew?" She says my name and my dick twitches again. It hasn't calmed since I saw her half-naked. Her voice brings it back to full mast. "Where are you?"

"I just got to my building. I'm heading up to my apartment." I arch a brow at the doorman. "I wanted to see if you're in the mood for a burger at your favorite place."

I hear the distinctive sound of rustling. "What? You're in New York? You're not coming home for another few days."

"I'm back early. Can I swing by and pick you up after I shower?"

"Actually," she begins on a small, soft laugh." Sydney is having a party tonight. I'm at your place. I needed the peace and quiet. I hope that's okay."

It's perfect.

"I'm about to walk through the door. I hope you're decent." I shoot the doorman a wide grin. The look of confusion on his face is pure gold.

She exhales deeply. It's breathy, light, and fuck is it sexy. "I am."

"I'll see you in less than a minute."

"Crew?"

My heart stops at the sound of my name from her lips. There's a need in her voice I've never heard before. "Yes?"

"I'm glad you're back."

"Me too," I say quietly in return before I start back toward my apartment, ready to face the woman

61

TROUBLEMAKER   *Deborah Bladon*

I'm going to fantasize about every fucking day until I draw my last breath.

Chapter 11

Crew

I stare into Adley's vibrant blue eyes. I see things now that I couldn't see when I was standing over her near naked body imagining what it would be like to touch her.

Her eyes are red, her bottom lip is swollen. She's been sobbing and biting on that lip. It's what she does when her world has fallen off its axis. The thought of her alone, on my couch, crying herself to sleep breaks my heart.

"I didn't know you were coming back." She tugs on the bottom of the white T-shirt she's wearing. She also slipped a pair of cut-off denim shorts over her panties.

Her hair is a mess and her face scrubbed clean of makeup. It seems impossible, but it makes me want her even more than I did ten minutes ago.

"My work was done." I brush past her to take my bags to my bedroom. "I have things to take care of here."

Her. I want to take care of her.

I hear the soft pad of her bare feet as she follows me down the long corridor to my master suite. It's tucked away from the main living area and the guest room.

I flick on the lights and my eyes are instantly drawn to my bed. My pillow is missing. I smile inwardly with the realization that she came in here to get it before she sprawled out on the couch.

TROUBLEMAKER   *Deborah Bladon*

I drop everything on the bench at the foot of my bed and turn back to face her. She's tiny when she's not wearing heels. She looks vulnerable and broken. I want to take her in my arms, but I can't. I've always let her come to me when she needs my broad shoulders to cry on.

"I'm going to shave and take a shower."

Her eyes land on my jaw. "You look different like that."

I rub my hand over the layer of stubble. "Different good or different creepy?"

She studies my face for a long second. "Good."

"The beard stays." I could stare at her for hours. I've wasted too many years not looking at her, now I can't tear my eyes away from her.

She dips her chin and looks down. "I can leave if that's better for you. Sydney's party must be winding down by now."

It's barely midnight. Sydney is twenty-one. The party is just hitting its stride. "You're staying the night."

She nods without complaint. "I appreciate that."

I shrug out of my suit jacket and toss it on the bed. "I gave you that key because I want you to come here when you need a place to crash. That hasn't changed."

Her eyes are glued to me as I tug the tail of my light blue shirt from my pants.

She clears her throat. "I have to leave for work early. I'll try to be quiet so I don't wake you. You must be exhausted from your trip."

TROUBLEMAKER   *Deborah Bladon*

"Are you heading to bed now?" I ask as I toe out of my shoes and slip my socks off.

"No. I mean if you are, I should too." Her gaze trails over my biceps and chest until it lands on my face.

I finger the second button on my shirt. The first is already undone. I tucked my tie into my jacket pocket somewhere over Kansas. "I'm going to shower, then have a drink. You're welcome to join me."

Tilting her head she looks toward the washroom that's attached to my bedroom. I wait for her to make a flirtatious joke about my unintentional invitation for her to shower with me. When she finally looks at me again, her expression is pained. "Did you have fun in Vegas?"

I swallow. "It was a work trip, Ad."

"It's Vegas. You must have fit in time for more than work."

"Not this trip." I unbutton the second button on my shirt. "I was all work and no play this time around."

She steps back, her eyes never leaving my hands. "I'll wait for you in the other room while you shower."

"I won't be long." I watch her walk away, a faint flicker of hope burning in my chest that those questions didn't come from just a friend, but from a woman who wants me as much as I want her.

***

TROUBLEMAKER   *Deborah Bladon*

"You can put that fucking puzzle back where you found it, Ad." I gesture toward the cardboard box with my tumbler of scotch. "That's not happening tonight."

She slides it an inch forward on the coffee table with the tip of her index finger. "I think tonight is a perfect night for us to try again."

The words get twisted in their delivery. I do want to try again. I want to try and redefine our relationship again. The first time we decided to be just friends, but that's not fucking working for me anymore.

When I exited the shower, my pillow was back where it belonged with the bonus of Adley's fragrance attached to it. That means she walked into my bedroom when I was in the shower. The bathroom door was wide open. One turn of her head and she could have seen me through the glass walls of the shower. Granted, it steamed up pretty quickly, but I like the idea of her wanting to see me nude. Whether that's reality is for me to find out.

"Let's play a game." I move to sit on the couch.

Her eyes skim over my bare chest the same way they did when I walked into the kitchen wearing only black silk pajama bottoms to pour myself a drink. I saw her topless so I thought I'd return the favor.

Her hardened nipples thanked me for the show, even if she didn't.

She draws her knees to her chest in the leather chair she's sitting in that's next to the couch. "What game?"

TROUBLEMAKER   *Deborah Bladon*

I take a large swallow of scotch before I look at her. "Truth or Dare."

She bites the corner of her bottom lip and my cock stirs. I take another sip to calm myself.

"Are you game, Ad?"

She nods softly. "I'm game. You go first."

Chapter 12

Adley

"What will it be?" He arches one of his dark brows. "Truth or dare?"

I'm tempted to go with the dare just to see what it would be. I felt something different in the air between us in the bedroom, but now I'm not sure if it was my imagination playing tricks on me or not.

When he called to say he was back home and on his way up to his place, I almost fell off the sofa. I ran into the guest room to put on one of the white T-shirts he keeps in there for me. I pulled the jean shorts I'd worn over to his place back on and ran my hands through my hair.

I made myself at home when I got here hours ago. It felt comfortable and right. Now, that he's back my world feels even more settled.

"Truth," I answer simply.

He narrows his eyes. "What was the last thing that made you cry?"

My heart stutters in my chest. I was crying earlier. The tears born from a sappy scene in a movie I was watching, but they quickly morphed into something else entirely. That's how it works with me. A spark of sentimentality ignites a blaze of sorrow deep within.

"A movie," I answer truthfully since that's what the rules of this game call for. "That's why it's called a tear-jerker. I couldn't keep it together through the first fifteen minutes."

TROUBLEMAKER   *Deborah Bladon*

"What was it about?" He keeps his gaze on me as he places the glass of liquor on the coffee table.

I glance down, tempted to swallow what's left. I can't. Not tonight. Courage has to come from within me. I want to know if what I felt in the bedroom was real. Crew's not going to be the one to make the first move. He values our friendship too much, maybe even more than I do.

"That's another question and it's not your turn," I point out with an unexpected calmness in my voice. It's not an accurate reflection of how I feel inside. I'm anxious, nervous and unsure of which direction this game is headed.

"I guess that means you're at bat," he quips.

The comment isn't lost on me. I know he has an issue with Trey. He has since that night at the club when he saw the two of us dancing.

"Truth or dare, Crew?"

He waits for a beat before he answers, his eyes skimming over my face. "Let's go with truth."

I hone in on the one topic I know he'll have a strong opinion on. I've never doubted Crew's honesty and I know he wouldn't answer this differently if I asked it outside the context of the game, but still, my curiosity is too strong to push the issue aside. "What do you think of Trey?"

He shoves a hand through his hair. He didn't style it after his shower and it's long enough that it's incredibly sexy when messy. He looks at me before his gaze drops to the floor. "Why? Are things more serious between you two than they were when I left?"

69

"You have to answer the question truthfully. You'll have your chance to ask me that if I pick truth next round."

His right knee bounces slightly with aggravation. I've seen it before. Usually that nervous energy is reserved for his family or a business deal gone astray. "Fine. I don't think he's good enough for you."

His protective nature has always been one of the things I like most about him. He's not just that way with me. It's the same with his sister and brothers. He has other friends, including women he'll do almost anything to protect too. "It's your turn at bat."

"Point taken, Ad. I'll drop the baseball references and you'll pick truth this round."

I don't argue. I know what the question is going to be and I want to answer it. Since we agreed to stay out of each other's personal lives, he's never questioned me about any of the guys I've been with. I have a feeling that's about to change now.

"Where are things between you and Hale?" he asks right on cue.

"We kissed."

"You kissed?" He leans forward to rest his forearms on his thighs.

"Yesterday," I answer quickly. "We had coffee and then when we said goodbye we kissed."

"So you're saying you haven't made it to second base yet?"

"You said no more baseball references and you were allowed one question, not ten."

TROUBLEMAKER   *Deborah Bladon*

He tosses me a small smile. "No more baseball references and just one more question for this round."

I sigh, knowing what it's going to be. "You're going to ask me how the kiss was."

He nods silently.

"It was fine."

"Fine," he repeats slowly drawing his top teeth over his bottom lip. "It was a fine kiss."

"It was a fine first kiss," I elaborate even though he didn't ask. "Not all first kisses blow your socks off."

"It depends who the first kiss is with." He cocks his head. Why does he look even more devastatingly alluring tonight?

My phone chimes, the tone loud since the volume is at its highest setting. "I need to look at that. I'm on call at the clinic."

He reaches to pick up the phone from where I left it on the coffee table. His eyes skim the screen before he hands it off to me. Then, in an instant, he's on his feet headed back into the kitchen without a word.

I look down and instead of feeling an ounce of disappointment, I feel relief.

It's a text from Trey.

My ex showed up at the game. We're headed back to her place. She swings both ways (get it?) so you're welcome to join us.

I type out a reply and hit send.

I'll pass. It's been fun, Trey but I think we should just be friends.

I lightly bite the nail of my thumb while I wait for his response. Crew still hasn't come back. I know he saw the text.

My phone chimes again and my gaze drops instantly to the screen.

I could use a good friend in this town. Friends it is.

I smile. Where there was once potential for more between us, now there's the foundation for friendship. I won't mourn that.

"Are you sticking around?" Crew walks across the room toward me. "I might have caught the tail end of Hale's text message."

"You read the entire thing."

"What's the verdict?" He scrubs the back of his neck with his hand.

I rest my phone on the arm of the chair I'm sitting in. "I'm going to hold out for a first kiss that blows me away."

"Does that mean it's over between you two?"

"We agreed to be friends." I don't want it to sound pathetic because it's not. There was a time in the past when I'd take it to heart if a man agreed to be just friends with me as easily as Trey did. Now, I cut my losses as soon as I realize the fit isn't right. "That means you better watch out, or he may inch you out of the position of my best guy friend."

"That won't happen." He settles back down on the couch, his hands falling to his thighs. "I'm not letting anyone take my place in your life."

I don't respond. I can't. A heated rush runs through me. I'm not imagining the way he's looking at me. Something has definitely shifted between us. I have no idea where this is going, but I want to find out.

Chapter 13

Crew

My turn.

A million questions are running through my mind now that Hale has suddenly dropped out of the picture. I saw the text. I have no idea if Ad is into what he proposed, but I was holding my breath in the kitchen waiting to see if she'd race out the door to be part of the Hale's babe threesome.

My mind took a second to catch up with the reality of what she said to me. It's over between her and Hale.

"Are we still playing?" Wetting her lips with a lash of her tongue she looks over at me.

How do I answer that? I'll play Truth or Dare with her all night, but I'm tired of edging around what's going on between us. That game needs to end tonight.

"What'll it be, Ad. Truth or dare?"

She hesitates, and I wonder if she's going to take the leap and take a dare. Before her text exchange with Hale, I would have kept the dare clean. Now I'm not so sure.

"Truth," she answers without hesitation.

"You mentioned your first kiss with Hale." That pinch on my last nerve that I felt every single time I said or heard his name isn't there anymore. Now, he's just another guy who passed through her life. The chemistry was never there. I could sense it at

TROUBLEMAKER   *Deborah Bladon*

the burger place. A fuck between them would have been just as boringly fine as the kiss.

"Are you still talking about him?" As she stretches the bottom hem of her T-shirt rides up to expose her stomach. "Do you want his number? Maybe you and Trey can be friends too. We can all hang out."

I like that she's teasing me. She's pushed aside whatever sadness she was feeling earlier. She's happy. I still crave the knowledge of what brought her to tears, but she'll come to me with that if and when she wants to.

"Hale and I will never be friends." I smile wryly. "I was just about to ask about the first kiss you ever had."

Her eyes widen. "Like ever?"

I lean back on the couch, watching her reaction. "Tell me about your first kiss. How old were you? What was his name?"

She answers so quickly that I know that it's a good memory. She's held onto the details tightly. "I was eleven. His name was Tommy Marshall. It was an amazing first kiss."

I inhale deeply. This is what I want more of. I want to know what she was like when she was a kid and who her friends were. I want every detail about anything that ever mattered to her.

"It happened after school," she goes on as she runs the palm of her hand over her knee. "He asked me to meet him. I didn't know why, but I liked him so I thought I should go. When I came around the corner, he was already there. He dropped his backpack, grabbed my face and kissed me."

75

It's the stuff young girl's dreams are made of. I want to thank Tom for giving her the gift of that kiss. She deserves to be wanted that way every day of her life.

"It sounds like Tom was a catch."

"We held hands and kissed a few more times." She looks past me to the distant lights of the city. "I sometimes wonder where he is now. I hope he's happy."

If he's got that same memory to fall back on, he's doing all right.

"Truth or dare, Crew?"

I'm not about to tarnish her answer with a dare to do something she's not ready for. I opt for the safe choice. "I'll go truth again this round."

There's a hint of challenge in her eyes when she looks at me. She takes a deep breath. "What was your first time like?"

Hell if I can remember that far back. I probably kissed a girl when I was in the second or third grade. That memory has gotten buried under everything else I've done with the female population since I realized how intoxicating a woman's lips and body are. "I don't remember who my first kiss was with, Ad."

She runs her fingers through her blonde locks, her eyes never leaving mine. "I wasn't asking about your first kiss, Crew. I want to know about the first time you fucked a woman."

My heartbeat quickens and my cock hardens. She just slid a toe over the line we swore we'd never cross. I'm ready to pick her up and carry her over it. I

TROUBLEMAKER *Deborah Bladon*

give her one last out because if we're doing this, I'm all in. "You're sure you want to go there?"

She holds her breath for a beat before she answers. "I want your truth about your first time. Tell me."

I reach forward to gulp down the last swallow of scotch in my glass. I should pour another but I have to stop with that shit. I've been using it as a crutch for too long. It's a decent way to hide from reality but tonight I want to be present. I want this question to lead to more.

"I was seventeen. She was older. It was good as far as first times go."

"How much older?" she asks immediately, both her brows shooting up.

"Five years." I drum my fingers over my thigh. "She was the older sister of a friend. It was winter break, so she was home from college."

"You'd already done stuff with girls before though, right?"

When I was a teenager, I ate pussy like I was a dying man and it was my last meal. I never took it beyond that though, because the girls were always willing to drop to their knees to reciprocate. After blowing my load, I'd pack up and head out or send them home.

It wasn't until I met Jenna that I felt the urge to bury my dick in anyone.

"The usual stuff teenagers do." I smile. "I was never short of female company in high school."

That earns me an eye roll. "I can imagine what you were like. The girls must have been lined up to be with you."

TROUBLEMAKER   *Deborah Bladon*

I would have pushed them all aside for her, but back then she was too young for me. She was also too blonde. My draw to dark-haired women has always been there. It's not that I've never bedded a golden-haired beauty or a redhead. I have, too many times to count.

I fell into a pattern with brunettes. I'd choose one and then another would be waiting her turn. At some point, I just narrowed the playing field by looking for the first available beautiful brown-haired woman who showed an interest in me. I'd approach her, buy her a drink and by the time the proposition left my lips, she'd be wet and ready.

"I wasn't good to women back then," I say that like I'm the poster boy for how to treat a woman now. I'm not. I try my best to be a decent guy after I've been with a woman, but it doesn't always go as planned.

"Why not?"

"I had a big appetite after I fucked Jenna." I don't break eye contact with her. "I wanted more and I didn't stop."

"You haven't stopped," she corrects me quietly.

Wrestling with disappointment in myself I don't respond immediately. Even though we never talk about who we're fucking she knows I go through a steady stream of partners on a monthly basis. Occasionally, I'll settle into a pattern with a woman for a few weeks, but it doesn't last. I never want it to.

"I'm not judging." Her mouth twitches. "It's not like I'm a saint."

TROUBLEMAKER   *Deborah Bladon*

I bow my head down. I don't want to know about her past. I don't think I can stand hearing about how many men have tasted her pussy or fucked her. The thought of her mouth on another man's dick creates a knot of jealousy in my chest.

This was so much easier when I saw her as just a friend. It started to shift on New Year's Eve when she ditched her date to take care of me. My feelings for her have only intensified since then. I sat next to her at Nolan's one Sunday in February. The smell of her perfume permeated my skin. I went home and jacked off thinking about her.

The guilt wore on me, so I shifted my focus. I fucked other women, drank more and when she showed up on my doorstep the night of the snowstorm I let her in. We watched television and shared a beer. It was light and easy but when she went to bed, I thought about her lips wrapped around my cock.

I'm a strong man but I have a limit and I'm barreling toward it at full speed.

"I'm going to get a bottle of water." She pushes to her feet. "When I get back it's your turn. Think about whether it's going to be a truth or a dare."

I eye her sweet ass as she walks into the kitchen. All bets are off. It's time to dare Adley to show me how she really feels.

Chapter 14

Adley

I use my time in the kitchen to drink half a bottle of water and calm my nerves. I didn't know how Crew would react when I asked him the question about his first time, but he hesitated only briefly before he answered.

I can feel that we're edging toward something more intense than the *just friends* arrangement we agreed to after we first met. The thought of losing Crew as a friend scares me, but not taking a chance when there could be something more between us, terrifies me even more.

Crew Benton is without a doubt, the once-in-a-lifetime type of man all women dream about.

"Did you fall asleep in there?" There's amusement in his tone as he calls from the other room.

I adjust the hem of the T-shirt I put on. I wish I would have had more time to get ready before he walked through the door. I didn't expect to see him tonight, so I wasn't exactly worried about what I looked like.

I round the corner and walk back toward where he's sitting. I feel his eyes on me when I lower myself on the sofa next to him.

It's a risky move, but I want this.

"Do you want to keep playing, Crew?" I look over at him. He stretches, resting his arms on the back of the sofa. My eyes trail over his chest and tight abs

TROUBLEMAKER   *Deborah Bladon*

before they land on the front of his pajama bottoms. The outline of his erection is clearly visible.

"Truth or dare?" His voice is deeper; the tone gruff.

I turn so I'm facing him, my leg bending at the knee as I rest it on the sofa. I know I'll likely regret this in the morning, but life isn't all about playing it safe. I've done that for the past few years and look where it's gotten me.

"What will it be?" He tilts his head, studying the spot where the tattered hem of my jean shorts meets my thigh.

"Dare."

"Kiss me."

My head shoots up. I stare at him but he's still focused on my body. His gaze is now carving a path over my pebbled nipples. "You want me to kiss you?"

"I dare you to kiss me." He makes the subtle correction with a tilt of his chin as his eyes meet mine. "We talked about memorable first kisses. I'm daring you to see how memorable my kiss is."

The sly smile that curves his lips only makes me want to taste them more.

"What do you say, Adley?" he whispers roughly as he leans closer. "Are you up for the dare?"

I'm not one for backing down from a challenge. The consequence of what I'm about to do bears down on me, but I don't care.

I move quickly, my legs sliding over the soft leather of the sofa before they straddle him. I land in his lap, his lips closer to mine than they've ever been.

His hands dart from the sofa's back to my thighs. He pins me there, pushing me down so I can

81

feel the steely length of his cock pressing into me through the barrier of fabric that separates us.

I raise my hands tentatively, twisting my fingers through his hair. It's as soft as I imagined. A brief image of his face between my legs while I yank gently on the strands invades my thoughts. I pull lightly, tilting his head until his lips align perfectly with mine.

His eyes are hooded, dark and full of the restless need I feel inside of me.

"I accept the dare," I whisper against his cheek before I move to cover his mouth with mine.

His lips part to invite me to taste more. Our tongues collide instantly, lashing against one another. He groans into the kiss, his hips grinding up to meet my body, the movement an invitation for me to take what I want.

I slide myself along the length of his thick cock, shivering when I hear the low moan that comes from his throat.

I've never been kissed like this before. It's exquisite, indulgent, intoxicating. I want it to last forever. It makes me dream of more, and touches that are only from him; his fingers, his mouth, his cock.

"Jesus," he hisses the word out as he moves. His hands slide to cup my ass before he flips me over in one swift movement. My back lands on the soft leather and suddenly he's hovering above me, one strong hand pinned to the back of the sofa to support his weight.

"I. Want. More," he growls against my mouth as his hand inches up my stomach.

I don't stop the kiss or his hand. I can't. Every inch of me that is blessed with his touch feels alive. I've never felt this desired before. I'm so wet that I know he can feel it through my shorts. He has to know what he's doing to me.

I arch my back to show him that I want everything he does.

He deepens the kiss, his tongue moving as slowly as his hand. It's an achingly delicious path to a place I've only imagined in my mind.

I feel his fingers when they glide along the underside of my right breast. I moan because I can't control what my body wants. The sound brings a smile to his lips that I feel through the kiss.

There's nothing between us but pure lust and need.

For the first time in a long time, I feel safe and wanted.

"Crew." His name escapes my lips in a low hum when I feel his fingers on my nipple.

He pinches it so hard that I yelp.

"Dare me to do more." The raw need in his voice draws goosebumps to my skin.

I stop him with a hand to his chin. I look into his eyes. They're the same mesmerizing eyes that I've seen for the last two years but they're reflecting back differently to me now. The hunger that I see in his gaze is a perfect match to what I feel inside.

"Crew," I murmur again, while I struggle to think of the right words to say. I want him to strip me bare and take me to his bed.

"I'll take care of you." His gaze travels slowly over my face. "Let me show you."

TROUBLEMAKER   *Deborah Bladon*

I nod. I've never wanted anything more in my life than to make love to this man.

Just as his hand trails over my stomach, he pulls back suddenly, rushing to get to his feet. His abrupt movement and the loud music that fills the room catch my breath in my throat. I reach for him to steady myself but he's not there. Even though I'm on my back on the sofa, I feel as though the entire world is falling away beneath me.

"My phone," I mumble as my mind catches up to what's happening. "That's my phone."

It's in his palm before I'm upright. I take it from him, our fingers touching briefly.

"Adley York," I answer breathlessly. "What is it?"

I listen intently as a female voice from the answering service for the clinic explains something to me about a dog and an accident.

"I'm coming," I tell her calmly. "I'll be there in fifteen. I'll call Dr. Hunt myself."

When I look up, Crew's not there. The only reminder of what we just did is the tenderness of my lips, the ache in my core and the feeling that I just made one of the biggest mistakes of my life.

TROUBLEMAKER   *Deborah Bladon*

Chapter 15

Crew

I had to leave the room after she took that call. It was the only thing I could do to stop myself from grabbing her phone and tossing it out a window.

I was so close, so fucking close to being inside her.

"Crew?" Ad's voice carries down the long hallway to my bedroom. I came in here to get dressed. I put on a pair of jeans and a gray T-shirt. If she's leaving at this time of night, I sure as hell am going with her. "Crew, I need to go."

I'm out of the bedroom like a shot. I jog down the corridor with unlaced shoes. "Wait. I'm coming with you."

She turns to look at me. Somehow she's been able to get into her scrubs, tuck her hair into a messy bun and pack up her stuff in record time.

"No," she says flatly. "I can get there on my own."

"I'll get a car to take us." I walk over to the table where I left my phone. I'll call Bill. He'll be here in less than ten minutes.

"I ordered an Uber." She waves her phone at me. "He's around the corner. I have to go now."

I don't want this. Her fingers are dancing all over the front of her neck which means she's already regretting what happened on my sofa. The nervous energy bouncing off of her is palpable.

"Let me come with you so we can talk in the car," I offer because desperation is settling in my gut and I need it gone now. I won't let her walk out of her thinking she's made a mistake.

She bows her head to look at the phone's screen. "He's almost in front of the building."

"Ad." I take a step toward her. "We need to discuss what happened."

She slips her backpack over her shoulder. "We don't. It was a game. We were playing a game."

"Don't." I exhale in a rush. "Don't say it was just a game. You know that what happened was more than that."

Her intense blue eyes skim over my face. "I don't have time to talk about this."

She didn't completely shut me down. I take that as a win right now. "When can we talk?"

She inches backward toward the door. "Tomorrow?"

"When? What time?" With every measured step she takes, I match it with one of my own.

"I have to work."

"After work then?"

She nods. "I'll be done at five."

"I'll be outside the clinic at four-fifty-nine."

The frown that covers her lips eats at my heart. "I'll go now."

I ache to follow her out, but I don't. I stand in silence as she opens my apartment door and walks out alone.

***

TROUBLEMAKER   *Deborah Bladon*

I sit back in my chair and listen intently as the manager of our flagship store explains away the staffing issues that she has yet to get a handle on.

"Miriam," I interrupt, because excuses have no place in my office. The people who work for me know this. I don't have the time or the inclination to listen to the mundane details of why something unacceptable has happened. "Clearly, you're not manager material."

She blows out a rush of air. "I disagree, Crew."

Of course she does. This is the third time in as many months that she's been sitting across from me giving me some bullshit reason for why we're running through sales staff at warp speed. "Explain to me why you've had three sales associates quit this month."

"I was explaining that." It never fails to amuse me that just because a person is older than I am, that they believe that's an automatic pass. Miriam is fifty-five. She came highly recommended by her last employer, a competitor whose annual sales are less than a quarter of ours.

Taking her on based on her stats on paper was a no-brainer. She's proving that I need to rethink the hiring process. "You were making excuses; poor excuses."

"What do you want from me?" She slides forward a touch in her chair. She's not going on the offense. This is a defensive move all the way.

"An explanation."

"People quit their jobs all the time." She rests her hands in her lap, a sign she's feeling somewhat confident that she'll be walking out of here with her job. I'm much less optimistic.

"Turnover has increased more than seventy-two percent since you took over the store." Statistics are my closest ally when I'm taking someone to task for their underperformance. "You're going to need to do better than trying to blame it on the fickle nature of your employees."

I'm getting to her. I sense it in the way she keeps looking at my closed office door. It's her escape route. She has no idea that I have to be out of here within the next three minutes in order to make it to where I need to be at five o'clock.

"I increased sales quotas, Crew. You had the bar set so low that virtually anyone could meet their monthly requirement. "

"You did what?"

She sighs heavily. "I gave them the choice to resign or be fired when they couldn't make their number. Obviously, the majority of them made the right choice and resigned. The rest I had to let go. If you're not pushing those girls to work harder, you'll never see an increase in your bottom line."

"Did I miss the memo that gave you the authority to change those numbers?" I glare at her.

"I did it over at Emblem Cosmetics. No one there seemed to mind one bit."

"Then I'm sure they'll be glad to have you back on board." I stand and button my suit jacket. "You'll be given a month's severance, Miriam. Your last day officially ends in twenty minutes. Leave your keys with my assistant."

TROUBLEMAKER   *Deborah Bladon*

"I'm fired?" She huffs out a humorless laugh. "You're seriously firing me for trying to improve your sales numbers?"

"I'm firing you for chasing away some of the best sales associates we've had."

"Of course you'd think that." She stands and slams her hands on the top of my desk. "Every man in this business thinks with his dick first. I bet you've slept with most of the women who left. Is that what this is about?"

"I'm going to ignore that," I say calmly, although I'm anything but. I keep my hands off the women who work for me. That's a powder keg that I want no part of.   "Leave, Miriam."

"Fine." She pulls the store keys from the pocket of her black pants and drops them on my desk. "I'll go work for your father. He offered me a managerial position at one of his sales offices a month ago. I should have known then that he was the only Benton worth answering to."

"Godspeed, Miriam," I quip as she walks out of my office. "You're about to enter the lion's den."

Chapter 16

Adley

Crew said he would be waiting for me outside the clinic at five o'clock. He didn't tell me that he wouldn't be alone. Ellie is next to him with Jonas holding tightly to her hand.

"Hey, Bean." I approach where the three of them are standing. I look down at Jonas. For a five-year-old, the kid has some major height. "What are you two doing in this part of town, kiddo?"

"Aunt Adley, you know why we're here." He rolls his eyes.

I have no idea why they are here. None.

"I thought you'd change before you left the clinic." Ellie scrunches her nose as she looks at my scrubs. "I guess this means you want to stop by your place first?"

I look at Crew for any hint, but he's silent and staring at me. *Great.*

It's been a long day. I'm cranky and tired. On top of that, I'm still trying to wrap my head around what happened between Crew and me last night.

The kiss was exactly what I wanted until we were interrupted. By the time I'd finished with the call from the clinic's answering service, the weight of what we'd done hit me full force. I jeopardized one of the most important friendships I've ever had. It was reckless. It can't happen again, even if my lips still feel tender and the ache for him has only intensified.

TROUBLEMAKER   *Deborah Bladon*

"We ran into Crew down the block." Ellie pats him on the back. "I'd invite him to join us, but he has to sit this one out since I only have three tickets."

Three tickets to what?

I scroll through my memories trying to latch onto anything that will clue me in to what the hell I had planned for tonight.

"You're obviously in a good mood," she says sarcastically when Crew doesn't make the expected comment about being left out in the cold. "Did you fire someone or something?"

"I did." He answers without taking his gaze off of me. "Miriam."

"You fired Miriam?" There's no mistaking the shock in Ellie's tone. "Does Nolan know? He loves her."

"He'll get over it."

She shakes her head. "He won't be happy."

He finally turns to look at her. "He will get over it, Ellie."

"So you haven't told him yet?"

Crew folds his arms across his chest. "I'll go to your place now and tell him face-to-face since it seems that my plans for this evening have fallen through."

"Can we go, Mom?" Jonas jumps in place. "I need to use the bathroom."

I jerk a thumb at the clinic. "Use the one in the waiting room."

Ellie takes a step forward before Crew stops her with a hand on her shoulder. He squeezes it. "Have fun tonight, Bean." Then he crouches and extends his closed fist to Jonas who goes in for a

91

TROUBLEMAKER   *Deborah Bladon*

hearty fist bump. "I'll bring you some pretzels this week, Joe."

"Those chocolate covered ones?"

He messes Jonas's blonde hair before he stands upright. "An entire bag just for you."

With that Ellie scoops her son's hand back into her own and they head into the clinic leaving me alone with the man I've thought about all day.

***

"It's the circus," I mutter after seeing a taxi top display for the big top as a cab waits at the red light on the street in front of the clinic. "We're going to the circus."

"I'm glad she didn't get me a ticket." He steps closer to me. "I'm not a fan."

I'm not either but I remember four or five months ago when tickets to a fundraising circus in Brooklyn went on sale. Jonas was on board immediately, and since May had no interest in going, he invited me personally during a phone call. My heart melted and I agreed straightaway.

"I take it you forgot about your plans with them tonight," he goes on. "I'm disappointed, Ad. We need to talk."

We do but I have to admit that I'm grateful for the reprieve. I haven't had a chance to take a breath since I was called in late last night. Dr. Hunt had to perform emergency surgery on a Bassett Hound that was struck by a car. I assisted and by the time we were done, the clinic was opening for the day.

TROUBLEMAKER   *Deborah Bladon*

I could have left early but I need the overtime so I stuck it out.

"I know," I say quietly. "We'll talk, Crew. It just can't be tonight."

His jaw tightens. "I don't want to put this off. This is important. I can stop by your place once you're home."

I'm too tired for this. I have to think through what I want to say before we have a discussion of this magnitude. I want to salvage our friendship. That's my main goal at this point.

I turn toward him and shrug. "I don't know what time it will be over. I think we should agree to talk tomorrow night."

"I have plans tomorrow night," he says curtly. "I can make it at lunch if that works."

Although I want to ask about his plans, I don't. This is the very reason why last night should never have happened. My emotions will get tangled in knots if we take things any farther. The idea of him with another woman is already tugging on my last nerve. I can't imagine hanging out casually at Ellie and Nolan's place with him after we've fucked and decided to try to be just friends again. It won't work.

"I can't do lunch." I look over when the clinic door opens and Jonas bounces out with Ellie right behind him. "We're having a going away party at noon tomorrow for one of the lab techs. It's her last day."

I don't know why I explain that to him. He didn't elaborate on his plans.

93

TROUBLEMAKER   *Deborah Bladon*

"Are you ready to go?" Ellie wraps her arm around my shoulder. "Someone is super excited to have some popcorn."

"I'll call you tomorrow, Ad," Crew says with a sigh. "I hope the three of you have a blast."

"We will," Jonas answers for all of us. "See you later, Crew."

"Later," he responds without looking at Jonas.

I still feel his eyes on me as we start off down the block to the car and driver waiting for Ellie and Jonas. I want to turn back, but I don't. I'm scared that if I do, he won't see his best friend. He'll see just another conquest and that's not who I am.

Chapter 17

Adley

I was roused out of bed just before one o'clock by the clinic's answering service again. This time it was a cat that had gotten itself into a sewing kit. It wasn't pretty.

The woman who owns the cat was frantic by the time I met her at the clinic. Dr. Hunt arrived shortly after I did and once again, we took care of the emergency side-by-side.

"Did you get any sleep at all, Adley?" He walks into the exam room that I'm prepping for his next patient. "Not to be rude, but you look like you haven't slept in a week-and-a-half."

I feel like I haven't.

The circus was over by nine, but instead of going home to bed, I hung out on Ellie's sofa. We drank virgin daiquiris and talked about our high school days. It was fun, and I needed the time to unwind with her, but I didn't get into bed until shortly after eleven so the unexpected wake-up call was rough.

"It's not considered rude if it's the truth, Donovan."

"Do you want to head home?" He stands back and looks me over. "You can take the rest of the day off."

It's a generous offer, but my pay is based on my presence in this place. I can't just leave. If I do that, I'll lose out on enough money to feed me for a week. "I can stick it out."

"We'll compromise." He turns to look at the cabinet that's against the wall. "You'll stay for Kim's going away party and then you'll clock out at five."

How is that a compromise? My shift ends at five.

I watch as he picks up a small bottle of vaccine before he places it on the metal tray next to the exam table. "You forgot to scan your security badge when you left today, Adley. I'll make a note on the schedule that I send to payroll that you didn't leave until five on the dot."

I get an afternoon off with pay.

"I'm forgetful like that." I bite back a grin.

He doesn't hold back as his mouth curves into a smile. "Next week let's meet to talk about school. You up for that?"

I nod. We circle this same topic every couple of months. I knew he'd bring it up any day now. He hasn't made a secret of the fact that he assumes I'll take the same path as Antonella, a woman who used to work here and will be again in two years. She left as a vet assistant and will be returning as Dr. Javier.

"Let's get our patient in here so we can give Kim the farewell party she deserves." He scans the tablet in his hand. He has no idea that a big part of me wishes that goodbye cake in the lunchroom had my name written on it.

**

TROUBLEMAKER   *Deborah Bladon*

"You scared me." I rub the ache in the middle of my forehead. "Never do that again."

Crew takes a step back. "I'm sorry. I didn't mean to scare you. Your reaction scared the hell out of me."

I was walking toward my apartment listening to music with my earbuds in when two large hands grabbed my shoulders from behind. A knee to the groin was part of my instinctive reaction to protect myself. The quick drop of his hands to cover himself was part of his.

There's no way I could have known it was Crew behind me. The man has a stronger work ethic than I do. I would never have expected to see him in the middle of the afternoon, especially in front of my building.

"I hope I didn't hurt you." I wince.

He looks down at the front of his gray pants. It's hot out today and yet he looks cool and collected in his suit. The black button down shirt underneath and the sunglasses still resting on his nose give him just enough of an edgy look to draw the attention of most of the women passing by us on the sidewalk.

"It's still in workable order."

He's referring to the fact that he's semi-hard beneath his pants. I can see that for myself.

How do men do it? How do they wander through their day with their cocks springing up to say hello whenever they damn well please?

"I called out to you." He fingers one of the earbuds that I pulled out when I realized who I was trying to maim. "When you didn't answer I thought a tap to the shoulder would do the job."

97

TROUBLEMAKER   *Deborah Bladon*

"What job? To get yourself killed?"

He laughs a little. "I have no doubt you could kill me if you wanted to, Ad. I hope that it's not part of your agenda after the other night."

The other night. I'm still trying to process that. An afternoon nap would help me do that.

"The only thing on my agenda right now is sleep."

"You're not making a pit-stop here? You're skipping work to take a nap?" He takes off the sunglasses and his eyes cut through me. "Are you feeling all right?"

"I was called in again last night." I pull the cord from the earbuds out of my phone. "Dr. Hunt let me leave early today."

He stalks closer, the expression on his face indecipherable. "Are you busy tonight?"

"You have plans," I point out.

"With my sister," he explains with a sigh. "I can be free of that by ten. If you sleep now, you'll be up by then, right?"

I feel like I could sleep for a week, but I know I won't. I'll get in a few hours and that will be sufficient until late tonight.

"I just want to talk, Ad. We can meet for a drink. You pick the place."

I'm surprised that he didn't immediately suggest his club but that comes with a myriad of complications including all the women he intimately knows who hang out there on a regular basis.

They've never scared me away before and since we are still just friends, I see no reason to shy away now. "Veil East at eleven?"

TROUBLEMAKER   *Deborah Bladon*

His left brow twitches. "I'll be there. I'll have the manager close off the VIP area for us so we can discuss things in private."

I'm game. I don't like this awkward energy that's flowing between us. I want him to joke with me, kiss my hand and look at me the way he did before we played Truth or Dare.

"I'll see you tonight." I don't move from where I'm standing.

A slow smile blooms on his lips. "I'll count the hours, Adley."

Once he walks away, I turn back to my building. I catch Sydney walking out just as I'm about to walk in.

"Did you quit your job?" Her jaw drops. "You did it, didn't you?"

"No." I shake my head. Sometimes it's easier to tell an almost stranger your dreams and fears than it is those closest to you. I did that with Sydney early on and her confidence is something I know I can rely on. In some very narrow ways, she knows me better than Crew does, or even Ellie.

"I got the afternoon off," I go on, "I'm heading to bed for a well-deserved nap."

Her eyebrows lift. "You're in a surprise when you get up to our place, Ad."

"What surprise?" I ask suspiciously. I don't care what it is as long as it doesn't get between my bed and me.

"You know that super-hot friend you have? Black hair, green eyes and a fuck-me smile?"

"Crew?" I answer because seriously who else do I know who fits that description.

She nods. "He just dropped off a bouquet of insanely beautiful white lilies. He told me to put the vase by your bed because you love waking up to the smell of fresh flowers."

My bottom lip trembles. He knows that because the morning of the snowstorm I woke up in his guest room and noticed a vase of white lilies on the bedside table. When I asked him why they were there said he has his housekeeper bring in fresh flowers for both bedrooms twice a month.

I wouldn't shut up about how beautiful they were so he wrapped them up in an old roll of holiday paper and gave them to me to take home.

I kept them next to my bed until they all died a very slow and messy death.

"I wish I had a friend like him," she notes with a small smile. "You're so lucky, Adley."

I am. I just hope that what Crew and I had isn't lost forever.

Chapter 18

Crew

If I were the type of man who expected anything from a woman I would have been sorely disappointed this afternoon when Adley didn't call or text me to thank me for the flowers. I didn't hold my breath waiting for that to happen. It wasn't because I had three meetings and a photo shoot for our new lipstick line to manage.

It's because Adley York is old-school when it comes to thanking anyone for a gift. If she doesn't write out a thank-you note by hand, she delivers the words in person in the form of an enthusiastic hug.

As I watch her exit the elevator to the VIP level of the club, dressed in a sleek red strapless dress and matching heels, I already know what the first three words that pass over her pink-stained lips will be.

Thank you, Crew.

"Fuck you, Crew," she says as she approaches.

Why do I like those words so much more?

"It's good to see you too, Ad. You look like a dream."

"You're a nightmare."

She has no idea how badly I want her. Visions of me pushing her onto her back on one of the low tables and tasting her cunt get crossed with images of her bent over the metal railing that overlooks the crowded club while I inch up that dress and fuck her from behind.

"Did you skip the nap?"

That draws the corner of her mouth up in an almost smile. "I had a nap."

I wish I would have been invited along for that ride. If that were the case, she'd look a lot less rested, but much more satisfied than she does right now.

"Something's changed about you since this afternoon." I tap my index finger on my bottom lip. "Did you pick up a new attitude on your way over?"

I'm gifted with a full smile, perfect white teeth and all. This woman is beyond beautiful.

"You went to see Dr. Hunt today."

The man didn't waste any time. When I stopped by the clinic after seeing her, I asked him to keep our discussion private until I had a chance to tell Adley my plan, but so be it. There's always a workaround in my world.

"I did."

Her eyes rake over me stopping on my jaw. I shaved since I saw her this afternoon. Everything else is exactly as it was. Gray suit, black shirt, killer smile. I flash her one for good measure.

She scowls. "Why would you go behind my back like that? I need that job, Crew."

I lean my hip on the metal railing, briefly glancing over at the club below. We're as busy tonight as we are every other night. "You have that job, Ad. You're not going to lose it because you take some time off."

"I don't want to take time off." Her shoulders go back. "The clinic is short-staffed. I can't just skip out without a good reason."

TROUBLEMAKER   *Deborah Bladon*

My hand itches with the need for a glass of something. I bypassed the bar on my way up here and sent the VIP staff down to the first floor so I could spend time alone with Adley. I'm regretting that now. "You have a good reason for taking a long weekend. Besides, you weren't booked to work next Saturday or Sunday. Monday is technically the only day you have officially off."

My words do little to placate her. She's vibrating from anger or frustration, maybe a little of both. "Explain to me why you did it because from where I'm standing it feels like you're trying to fuck my life around."

I am. I'm trying to take her out of her comfort zone so she can see the world, and us, through fresh eyes. I look into her stormy blues.

"When's the last time you took a vacation?"

Her chin drops. I know the answer to that because I've been a constant in her life since shortly after we met.

Reaching out, I rest my index finger on her chin and draw it up, so she's looking directly at me. "I'll answer for you. It was when you went to Vegas to visit Ellie. That was two years ago, Ad."

She can't afford to travel. I've never offered to send her on the trip of her dreams because she'd push back with so much resistance that it would damage what we have. This time is different. We're hanging by a thread of something that neither of us can define.

"That was the last time," she agrees softly.

"My family owns a home in the Hamptons." I doubt like hell I've ever mentioned it to her before

TROUBLEMAKER   *Deborah Bladon*

because I haven't been there myself in years. "Take the weekend to go there and relax."

"The Hamptons?" Her face brightens. "Is it close to the ocean?"

"It's oceanfront. You can hear the waves as you fall asleep."

She shoots me a look. "Part of the deal is you going with me, isn't it? You want me to spend three days in a house all alone with you."

That's the plan although it's not quite as cut and dry as she thinks. "You'll be in the master suite. I'll take up residence in one of the other bedrooms. I'm going to head up there on Friday morning to get the place ready for you. I'll be there for the weekend too, but I'll need to work. That will give you plenty of time on your own. "

"You're working this weekend, but I'm not?" Her brows lift. "This is the problem, Crew. You think it's easy for me to tap out of work but you can't pull yourself away from your own."

I stare at her for a beat before I say anything. "I can work remotely. I have endless resources but bringing the clinic and all its patients to Westhampton Beach isn't one of them."

She rubs her hand over her mouth trying to hide a smile. "So you'll work and I'll sunbathe?"

A jolt of desires races through me at the thought of her in a bikini. That's a bonus I didn't consider when I hastily planned out this trip.

I saw how ragged she looked earlier. She's driving herself to the edge without a safety belt. This is a break that she needs. "You'll sunbathe, read,

TROUBLEMAKER   *Deborah Bladon*

swim in the pool, sleep, or whatever the fuck you want to do."

"Why are you doing this?" she asks with nothing but honesty in her expression.

"I don't think we can solve everything in this club tonight." I gesture to the dance floor with my chin. "This getaway will give us a chance to figure out where we stand. You'll have time to do your own thing. I'll cook for you and we'll come back here in a better place than we are now."

Her eyes meet mine. "I don't want to play Truth or Dare again."

I translate that to mean she doesn't want to kiss me again or do anything beyond that. I get it. If she felt the same insane hunger that I felt when our lips met, she's running scared. I'm not about to. I've never experienced anything close to that with a woman before. I want more. I know she does too. She can't mask her feelings as well as she thinks she can.

"You set the rules. I'm there to cook for you and hang out with if the mood strikes you."

Her lips purse. "I'll go, but I can do half the cooking."

I shake my head. "I need to come back to New York in one piece, Ad. Your talents are not in the kitchen."

She smiles that smile that tells me that I've got a chance. I'm taking it because if I don't, I'll regret it for the rest of my life.

Chapter 19

Adley

The other night after Crew invited me to a weekend away at his family's house in the Hamptons, I left Veil East. He didn't press to talk about things between us and I didn't either. The idea of spending time on a beach away from the city sounded like heaven.

The only communication we've had the past few days have been short text messages related to the trip.

He arranged to have a driver take me to the Hamptons. I'm in the car now and although I've spent most of the drive trying to focus on a novel my mom loaned me, I can't remember one word I read.

"Bill?" I call to the driver in the front seat. "Have you ever been to the Hamptons?"

He doesn't take his eyes off the road. "I've never been."

I scrunch my nose as I look at him in the rear view mirror. "I don't know what to expect."

"From what I've heard I think you should expect the opposite of Manhattan."

"So paradise, then?"

"Exactly." He nods briskly. "Use the time wisely. That's what I do every chance I get a break from the day-to-day."

I take a breath before I ask the same question I've already asked three times. "Are we getting close?"

TROUBLEMAKER   *Deborah Bladon*

"Closer than the last time you asked." He laughs. "Close your eyes, Adley. Dream a little dream and before you know it, you'll be standing in the doorway of Mr. Benton's home."

***

Holy shit.

I thought Crew's apartment was gorgeous. This place looks like it came out of a catalog for furniture that regular people can never afford.

I'm standing in the entry way with Bill by my side. He called Crew as we approached the winding driveway. I heard him agree to something and when he stopped the car and held open the door for me, I almost lost my breath.

The exterior of the house is breathtaking with shuttered windows and a wraparound deck. The inside surpassed that in spades when Bill opened the unlocked door and stepped aside so I could walk in.

The space is grand with vaulted white ceilings and dark wood beams.

Against the wall opposite the door is a fireplace framed with two large windows that overlook a sandy beach and the Atlantic.

A sitting area is to the right. There's a sofa and wingback chairs that are all light gray, with accessories in tans and navy blues that brings softness to the space.

Beyond that to the left is an open kitchen with a huge island and polished countertops that complement the white cabinetry.

I look around, taking in every perfect detail.

TROUBLEMAKER   *Deborah Bladon*

"Do you like what you see?" Crew's deep voice hits me from behind.

I turn to look at him.

My heart stutters for a beat.

He's wearing a thin white T-shirt and black shorts. His hair is wind-blown. He looks different out here away from the stress that sits on his shoulders in New York.

"It's a beautiful house," I say quickly to stop myself from commenting on how insanely hot he looks right now.

"I was out for a walk." He pats Bill on the shoulder. "You made good time. I wasn't expecting you for another thirty minutes."

Bill picks up my bags and brings them into the foyer. "It's early enough that the traffic was light."

It is early. Once I accepted the fact that I was taking the weekend off, I told Tilly. Between her coughing spurts, she offered to cover my shift from noon on if I agreed to do the same for her next Friday. Dr. Hunt signed off on it without question so I was ready to hit the road by one-thirty.

"Do you need me to come back to pick Adley up on Sunday, sir?"

I fidget on my sandal covered feet, the skirt of my white sundress dancing with the movement. I want to pipe up and say something, but the man works for Crew, not me.

"Crew," he corrects Bill with a smile. "We're heading back Monday and I drove up so you're off the hook."

Bill tosses him a wink. "Right, Crew, it is. If that's all, I'll head back."

TROUBLEMAKER   *Deborah Bladon*

"Drive safe." Crew dips his hands in the pocket of his shorts. "I don't have a dollar on me now, Bill, but I'll add it your tip when you take me to the airport on Tuesday."

Bill laughs like it's an inside joke. "Not a problem. You two enjoy the weekend. Remember what I said, Adley."

I nod. I remember exactly what he said. I'll use the time wisely. For the next three days it's me and casual Crew. I have a feeling I'm going to walk out of here a much different person than I am now.

Chapter 20

Crew

Being back in this house is a mind fuck. Seeing Adley in the foyer brought up a clusterfuck of emotions. My memories of this place aren't bad. They're not especially good either. Neutral is how I'd call it.

I splashed in the ocean with my siblings when I was a kid. My mom taught me how to drive a boat when I was fourteen. I hosted a party or two out here when I was in college but none of that has ever stay seared into my memory like the vision of Ad in her pure white dress with the ocean as a backdrop will.

If I could have stopped time for a beat, I would have just to take that in.

"What did Bill say that you're supposed to remember?" I ask as I pick up her bags.

She shoulders her large white purse. "He said to use my time here wisely."

She will. I'll make certain of that. "Time stands still out here. Before you know it, we'll be back on the road on Monday."

"You're going somewhere on Tuesday?" She looks down at the dark hardwood floor. "Is it back to Vegas?"

If Lucia had her way it would be. She wants an in person meeting now that she's pushing for full control of Veil West after my rebuff. I didn't peg her for a woman who would want to avenge a missed fuck, but her actions say otherwise. If the price is

TROUBLEMAKER   *Deborah Bladon*

right, I'll take her offer, but until now, she's tossing crumbs my way and I'm not biting.

"Boston," I respond quickly to ease her mind. "We've been scouting for a new Matiz location there. I have a tip on what might be a suitable space, so I'm heading there for a few hours to check it out."

For someone who regrets kissing me the other night, she's visibly relieved by my answer.

"Come with me." I inch a shoulder forward. "I'll show you to your sleeping quarters."

A laugh bubbles out of her at my lame attempt to do an English accent. "It's just a bedroom, right?"

She has no idea. "This way, Ad. Come see for yourself."

***

I left Adley in the master suite alone after I gave her the grand tour. The space is larger than her entire apartment. That was my mom's doing. She decided to have the house transformed from a six bedroom to a five to afford her more closet space and a bathroom that is ten times as big as it needs to be.

The only reason I readied that room for Adley is because it offers the best views of the ocean. I know she's never seen it in person. Ellie told me when I stopped by her place to drop off the bag of pretzels for Jonas.

I could see all the questions dancing in Ellie's eyes, but she didn't ask any. Instead, she said she was glad I was taking Adley out of the city for a few days. She sees the same cloud hanging over Ad that I have. Something has been brewing inside of her. Part of

111

that may be attributed to what happened between us at my apartment, but she's been carrying a burden for a long time. I'm hopeful that this weekend, she'll open up and share.

"Are there any other people here?" Adley's voice catches me by surprise. I've been standing in the main room looking out the window as day's light gives way to darkness.

I turn to look at her. She's showered and changed her clothes. The long black halter dress she has on suits her as does the style of her hair. Loose waves surround her face. "The caretaker was here when you arrived. I called him earlier this week to open the house back up."

Everything had been covered with heavy drop cloths until two days ago. When I got here this morning, there was still a lot to be done. Duncan, the caretaker, did his fair share but I took on the tasks of going to the market to get food, flowers and several bottles of red wine.

"The door was unlocked when we got here, so I was wondering if you were here alone." She looks me over. "I don't have to tell you how beautiful this house is."

It's a house. Beauty is subjective when your family has enough money to buy anything. I've never been impressed with my parents' wealth. I didn't understand when I was a kid that summers in a place like this weren't commonplace. I began to see the difference when I finally left private school when I was fifteen-years-old to go to public school.

That was a hard fought battle with my folks but I came out the victor. I'm glad. If not for that, I

TROUBLEMAKER   *Deborah Bladon*

never would have met Nolan or Adley, for that matter.

"I'm glad you agreed to come, Ad." I rake a hand through my hair. "I want you to make yourself at home. In the morning I'll show you the private boardwalk to the beach."

Her gaze darts to the descending darkness outside. "I'm looking forward to putting my feet in the ocean."

I want to push her to talk about what's going on between us, but I won't. I know she'll pitch the idea that we stay just friends but that's a road I can't go back down after tasting her lips and touching her skin. I'm fucking starving for more. She has to know that, even if she won't acknowledge it.

"Are you hungry?" I ask as I stare at her profile. "I can make us something to eat."

She smiles wryly when she turns back to me. "I'm famished. What's for dinner?"

Chapter 21

Adley

He cooked the most delicious steak I've ever had. I didn't tell him that because it would go straight to his head. The wine was exquisite too as were the baby potatoes and salad. The man has serious culinary talent. I already knew this from watching him in the kitchen at Ellie's. He's not against putting on an apron, rolling up his sleeves and getting dirty.

Dirty.

My mind flits back to a time when Ellie and I ran into a woman in a deli. Ellie was talking to her about Nolan while I was eavesdropping and I heard her mention how she'd fucked Crew in a photo booth in Times Square. She said it was the dirtiest sex she's ever had.

"Ad?"

I look at where his hand is perched in the air, holding the wine bottle. "Do you want more?"

I nod. "Sure, why not?"

He pours another quarter glass for me before he does the same for himself. "Where did you wander off to? You had a faraway look in your eyes."

I don't want to talk about his past sexual escapades in the heart of New York City, so I opt for something neutral. "Has your family always owned this house?"

"For as long as I can remember." His jaw tightens. I've become versed in the various ways Crew reacts when I bring up his family.

TROUBLEMAKER   *Deborah Bladon*

The only one I've ever seen him interact with is his younger sister, Lark. They're close. His two brothers and parents fall outside his inner circle, although he does see Kade for lunch at least a couple of times a month. I know that from Kade's confessional during our dinner.

He didn't go into too much detail about the inner workings of the dysfunctional Benton clan. He was cryptic about what had happened that pushed Crew to work at Matiz instead of at Benton Holdings, the family business.

I questioned Crew about it once, but he shot me a look that had enough force behind it to make my head spin.

"Do you want to go sit on the deck? We can listen to the ocean," he says huskily.

That's a tactile way to shut down a conversation he doesn't want to have about his family. I don't push because talking about mine isn't on the top of my to-do list either.

I stand in response, but not before he does. He pulls back the dining room chair and offers his hand. I take it because there's no reason why I can't touch him the way I always have.

My body would win an argument against that. The energy that flows between us when our skin meets is electric. I don't pull back though. I have to learn how to handle this if we're going to have any chance of salvaging our friendship.

"I'm glad you came up here, Ad." He tucks a piece of hair behind my ear the way he always does. It feels anything but ordinary tonight.

TROUBLEMAKER   *Deborah Bladon*

I'm not sure if I'm glad I made the trip yet. We're four hours in and we still have three nights and just as many days to get through. I need to make it out of this house with my heart in one piece and my friendship with him still intact.

"Take me to hear the ocean, Crew."

"Your wish is my command." He wraps my hand around his forearm and leads me to a set of glass double doors near the back of the kitchen.

When he opens them, the salty evening air, the sound of the ocean and his touch make me feel like I'm exactly where I need to be.

***

Last night went just as I thought it would. Crew and I sat on the deck outside and listened to the ocean before he had a call that tore him away. He hustled into the kitchen, closing the glass doors behind him and as I watched his hand fist around the edge of the granite countertop, I knew that it was time for me to call it a night.

When I walked into the house he pushed his phone against his chest to shutter our voices from whoever he'd been talking to. With a quick goodnight and an empty smile, he headed to the opposite side of the house where I assume he's still asleep.

A sliver of unfiltered light crept through a crack where the dark, heavy curtains in my room meet. It was enough to wake me from a full night's sleep. I haven't had that in months, maybe longer, and when I stretched out on the King size bed and listened

116

TROUBLEMAKER   *Deborah Bladon*

carefully, the only things I could hear were birds chirping and the ocean.

Coffee was what I craved so I went into the kitchen and used the French press and roasted beans to make myself a cup. A bowl of fresh berries and a scone were all I needed to enjoy a breakfast in solace on the deck off the kitchen.

Bill wasn't kidding when he said this place is the opposite of the city.

I'm in the main room now, looking over the selection of books that line the shelves that frame the fireplace. There are novels here that my mom would love to read. I take two pictures with my phone, so I can show her the next time I see her. Sending her any images from here would only result in a deluge of questions that I don't want to answer.

"Don't tell me that you've already had breakfast."

I turn to where Crew is standing at the open door to the deck. He's only wearing white board shorts. His entire body is peppered with moisture, his hair wet and stuck to the sides of his face.

The man is breathtaking.

"Fruit and coffee." I shrug with a smile. "Were you swimming?"

"There's no gym here." He pads across the hardwood floor with his bare feet. "I hit the pool to do a few laps. A few turned into more."

I admire his drive to push his body to its limits constantly. My work-outs are restricted to the time I spend on the sidewalks of Manhattan walking my way to a fatter wallet. Transportation isn't cheap in

117

the city and my legs are more than capable of getting me from point A to point B the majority of the time.

He scoops up a large white towel that was strung over the back of one of the chairs near the bookcase. I watch as he dabs it against his chest before rubbing it briskly over his hair. When he's done he looks even more devilishly handsome than he did when he first walked in.

"I have a conference call in fifteen minutes."

I should be surprised since it's Saturday, but I know that he's picked up the slack for Nolan since he married Ellie. Every Matiz location is open for business today which means Crew is the man to call if something doesn't go right. Delegation is not his strong suit.

"I think I'll sit on the deck and read." I point to the elaborate display of books. "These are real, right? They're not just covers set there to impress."

He huffs out a hearty laugh. "My mom would drop dead if she heard you asking that. Many of those books are first editions signed by the author."

I want to ask what the hell they're doing out here in nowhere land instead of in a glass case in the apartment his parents live in, but I just smile. I don't understand wealth. I've never had it and from where I'm standing it might offer an easier life in terms of worry, but it comes with the burden of expectation and stress. I have enough of that on my own small scale. Adding more money than I will ever need to that equation isn't appealing in the least to me.

"I'll take you down to the beach once I'm done." He reaches to scratch his knee, his bicep flexing with the motion.

TROUBLEMAKER *Deborah Bladon*

Why did I think this weekend was a good idea?

I don't know if he's trying to tempt me, but regardless it's working. I vowed I'd stick by my decision to keep things platonic between us, but he's not making it any easier.

"Good luck with that call," I say trying to keep my eyes on his face.

He knows I'm struggling. I see that in his soft smile and the cock of one of his dark brows. "Good luck with concentrating on your book, Adley."

Ass.

I try to look away when he turns to go back into the other wing of the house. I can't resist. He's gorgeous from every angle.

I'm less than twenty-four hours in and my inner strength is about to wave a white flag of surrender. I pick the first book my hand lands on and I head out to the deck with a mind full of dirty thoughts and an ache between my legs.

Chapter 22

Crew

Payback. That's what this is.

At least Ad could mask her arousal when she saw me this morning after my swim. I knew I got to her. Her nipples pebbled into high peaks under the pink dress she was wearing. She used the age-old tactic of crossing her arms over her chest to keep me from noticing. It didn't work.

I don't have the luxury of hiding my bulging erection. I'm wearing navy blue shorts and nothing else. It's still more than what Adley has on.

All that is covering her body is a red string bikini that looks like someone painted it on with precision. I may know what's underneath it now but I haven't got my first taste yet, and my cock is eager.

"You look happy to see me," she calls from where she's resting in a lounge chair near the heated pool. "You're smiling."

Little mynx.

"Not as happy as you are to see me." I slide my sunglasses down the bridge of my nose to peek over them at her bikini top.

"It's breezy out today," she lies.

It's hot as hell. The blustery weather from last week was a prelude to blue skies and a rising thermometer. I wouldn't have given a shit if we were forced to wear parkas on this trip. I wanted her alone and I got my wish. The bikini is a very welcome bonus.

TROUBLEMAKER   *Deborah Bladon*

She's coming around. That wall of protection she built around herself in my apartment the night we kissed is slowly breaking apart.

Patience is the key when it comes to Adley. That's one of the lessons I've learned since I met her.

Another is that she doesn't have a lot of close friends.

She treasures the ones she does and I'm on that list. Risking what we have scares the hell out of her. Truth be told, it scares me too.

"Did you take care of business?" she asks with her eyes closed.

"For now." I take a seat on the lounger next to her, impatience causing my shoulders to tighten. I want to ask her when we'll talk about what happened in my apartment, but she's relaxing at the moment; something that's been in short supply in her life in recent months.

She works herself to the bone for a salary that she can barely live on. She used to talk incessantly about going back to school to become a veterinarian but I've noticed in recent months that it's not a subject she willingly brings up. If someone else does, she seamlessly navigates the discussion in another direction.

I've asked her point blank if she's still interested in being Dr. York, she assures me she is.

"Why do you work so much?" She looks over at me. "You're super rich. Isn't there a point where enough is enough?"

It's never been about the money to me. My drive to succeed has a lot more to do with ego than it does wealth. I never wanted the silver spoon in my

121

mouth. I spit it out as soon as I was able to; branching out on my own to build a life that wasn't bound to my family.

Unfortunately, I still own a stake in their business. If it weren't for my mom, I would have sold it for pennies on the dollar years ago just to free myself of the burden of the twice yearly board meetings and back-and-forth bitterness between shareholders.

"I like the work," I admit as I drop my sunglasses on the small circular table between our loungers. "It's an adrenaline rush for me."

That answer doesn't satisfy her. Her brow furrows. "Don't you have enough excitement in your life outside of work? You don't have to chase the high by spending ninety percent of your time juggling the five hundred different businesses you run."

I laugh. "There's not nearly that many, Ad. I'm not a fucking robot."

"I know. Robots don't have hearts." She rests her hand in the middle of her chest between those two beautiful round globes of flesh I want to sink my teeth into.

"You think I have a heart?" I ask because it's a gateway to the discussion I've been ready to have since she walked through the door yesterday.

She looks down before her head turns toward the ocean. "You said you'd take me to the water when you were done with your call. That was five hours ago."

The subtle dig about my time spent on the crisis at the Matiz boutique in Los Angeles isn't lost on me. I had no intention of spending that much time

TROUBLEMAKER   *Deborah Bladon*

in the office I set up in Lark's old bedroom. I made over thirty calls trying to track down a shipment that had gone astray.

Customers were waiting in line at the boutique this morning anticipating a new lipstick and nail color combo. The manager didn't think to reach out to report that the shipment was M.I.A. until she unlocked the door of the store this morning.

I could have easily handed off the matter to someone at head office in New York to deal with but I welcomed the distraction. Spending time with Adley while we're not actively discussing where our relationship stands is becoming harder and harder for me to do.

"Do you think I have a heart, Ad?"

She swings her legs over the side of the lounger, so she's sitting and facing me directly. "Of course you have a heart."

I stare at her body remembering what it looked like on my sofa, lush and curvy; her skin smooth and creamy. "I know the last few days have been hell for you. They have been for me too."

Tilting her head, she studies my face. "What do you want, Crew?"

To strip you bare and fuck you until every cell in your body craves my touch.

"You know what I want, Ad." I stretch my legs, crossing them at the ankles. "I want you."

"You want to fuck me." It's not a question because we're beyond that. Nothing has changed for me since I kissed her. The driving need to be inside of her never lessens.

"Very badly."

123

TROUBLEMAKER   *Deborah Bladon*

Her eyelashes flutter as she drops her gaze. "If we did that, nothing between us would ever be the same again."

She's right. It would be impossible to go back to being just friends, but I'm well beyond that point already. I left my platonic feelings for her behind months ago.

"Is that such a bad thing?" I ask honestly. "We're adults, Ad. We can have sex and see where it goes from there."

"I know where it will go," she challenges, her hands fisting together in her lap. "We both know where it will go."

"Enlighten me." I stare at her. "Tell me where it will go."

"To hell." She stands suddenly, her hands darting to her hips. "Do you remember Gretel Gallant?"

"Who?" I run through names in my mind, trying to place that one.

"Gretel Gallant," she repeats slowly.

It's familiar but I can't place it. Guessing would only insult Adley more. Apparently, this Gretel woman is someone from my past. "Who is she?"

"A woman you fucked in a photo booth in a restaurant in Times Square."

I drop my gaze to my lap. Fuck my fucking past.

"What about Christy Marcus?"

I close my eyes before I shake my head.

"You fingered her to orgasm on a subway train before you took her to your place. I got to hear

124

TROUBLEMAKER   *Deborah Bladon*

all about that while I was cleaning vomit off her dog early one morning last year."

My head pops up. "How the fuck did my name come up during that?"

"You did it the night before she came into the clinic." She rolls her eyes. "How many black-haired, big-dicked men named Crew do you think finger women on the D-train on a nightly basis?"

How many women tell a veterinary assistant about their sex life?

"I can't erase my past." I look up at her face. There's a level of emotion in her eyes I've never seen before. "Don't punish me for that."

"I'm not punishing you." She moves to sit next to me, her outer thigh brushing mine. "I didn't bring up those women to throw them in your face."

"Why bring them up at all?" Uneasy, I draw in a deep breath. I don't know why I'm so surprised that she's heard about my encounters with other women. I've fucked women who sought me out based on what a friend told them about me. I didn't care what brought them to me. All I cared about was getting off.

Her hand reaches for mine and I greedily welcome the touch. I cup both my hands around hers as I rest them on my thigh.

"I want you to remember my name." Her voice is even and steady; a direct contradiction to the emotion in her eyes. They're filled with a mixture of confusion and despair. "A year from now, or five or ten, I want to be able to call you up and ask you to hang out. If we sleep together, I'm going to lose that. I don't know if either of us can handle life without the other anymore."

Fuck her and her common sense.

She's right, except she's not considering one possibility.

"Ad." I turn to the side so I can face her directly. I could drown in this woman. I want to. "It's not just about the fuck for me. There's more."

Her brows rise as she leans forward a touch. "More?"

"Yes," I say with a crack in my voice. I don't do this. I don't sit and discuss my feelings with anyone. I keep it all in, driving through my day with the ruthless force of a bull on a mission to crush everything in its path. Numb is how I want to feel twenty-four, seven. It's how I've always felt yet right now I want to tell her I'm feeling things I can't comprehend. They scare the hell out of me and make me feel safe at the same time.

"You're going to say that you'd never hurt me." She leans her head against my shoulder. "I know you wouldn't, Crew. You're one of the only people in my life that I know will protect me at all costs. That's another reason why we can't sleep together. I need you. I'm always going to need you."

My chest tightens with those words. They're brutally honest and a plea for me to back the fuck off so I can be the man she needs me to be.

Sacrifice isn't something I know, but I'll learn for her. I'll do it because losing her is a worse fate than never fucking her.

I need to stop tearing her up like this. I'll find a way to manage the need.

I inhale sharply. "You ready to check out the ocean, Ad?"

TROUBLEMAKER   *Deborah Bladon*

Her delicate hand flies to my chin, tilting it so I'm looking into her blue eyes. "We're good, right? You and I, we're okay?"

"We're good." I slide her hand to my lips and kiss her palm lightly, closing my eyes to chase away the thought that I'm never going to have more. Somehow, I have to accept that being this woman's friend is enough.

Chapter 23

Adley

I wasn't going to do it. I had no intention of pushing back on Crew that way until I started reading that damn novel I picked up from the bookshelf.

The main character was named Christy. That took me right back to that morning in the clinic when the beautiful tall black-haired woman had walked through the door with a puppy that had eaten its weight in mini bagels.

While I tended to her dog, she felt the need to explain why she wasn't at her place to watch over the dog while it was feasting on her intended breakfast. Crew's name popped up somewhere in the middle of her story about being on the subway. They'd just met. She draped her trench coat over her lap and his finger got busy on her magic button.

I didn't bring it up with him then, because it didn't matter to me. I was never oblivious to what went on his life even though he's always been oblivious to what's happened in mine.

It doesn't bother me that he's slept with more women than he can remember. He's a gorgeous man who loves to fuck. I bit back at the jealousy early on by dating other men. It always works, until it doesn't anymore.

I refuse to be just another name in his past. I don't want that. I won't be it. I brought up those other women because I want him to see that I fit into a

TROUBLEMAKER   *Deborah Bladon*

different corner of his life than any of them ever could. I'm not ready to give that up.

I can find another man to fuck. I can't find another friend like Crew.

The discussion was difficult, the moments spent on the beach afterward were awkward but it was all necessary.

We can go back to Manhattan in two days as friends. Eventually we'll both forget the kiss and life will be as it was.

It has to be. I need it to be.

"You're daydreaming about a burger, aren't you?" Crew steps into my line of sight as I turn from where I've been staring out the window. "You have that look in your eye again."

"What look?" I laugh through the question.

"The one that makes me want to grill you a burger." He looks out at the deck and the large silver grill that he used to cook our streaks. "I'm the Benton burger king."

"Is that supposed to be impressive?" I tease, grateful that the uncomfortable walk on the beach didn't carry into our evening.

He shakes his head, pointing his finger at me. "You're going to eat those words after I cook dinner for you."

"When is that happening?" It's barely six o'clock. I made a sandwich before I hit the pool and I saw Crew eating an apple less than an hour ago after we made our way back up the private boardwalk. I'm not hungry. I doubt he is either.

He glances down at his silver wristwatch. I haven't seen it on him since I arrived. I haven't seen

129

TROUBLEMAKER   *Deborah Bladon*

him in gray pants and a black button down shirt either but that's what he's wearing.

"After I get back." He runs his hand over his smooth jaw. He shaved since our walk. Showered too and applied what smells like Matiz cologne.

It's not lost on me that he's going somewhere alone. I ask because the curiosity is nipping at me. "Where are you off to?"

"I'm meeting a friend for a drink."

It's a woman. A man wouldn't warrant the effort he's put in to get himself ready.

"You have friends in the Hamptons?"

What an idiotic question. He has friends *everywhere*.

"She's visiting from Los Angeles." His gaze coasts past my face to the view of the ocean beyond. "We're not often in the same place at the same time."

Did you call her or did she call you?

I don't ask because I can't. I'm the one who retreated back to the friendship line less than three hours ago. Who he spends his time with is none of my business. He made a decision to forgo time with me tonight to spend it with someone else, just as I made a decision to keep things platonic between us. I can't be upset because he's doing what's best for him.

"Don't rush back," I say in a voice that doesn't sound like my own.

He caresses my lips with his eyes, hesitating briefly before he finally responds. "I'll be back in a couple of hours. Call if you need me."

I nod. I do need him but I won't call. I made the choice to let him go and now I have to watch him leave knowing he's on his way to meet someone else.

130

TROUBLEMAKER   *Deborah Bladon*

My heart breaks apart again. I'll put it back together. I always do. Maybe this time I'll get it right and Crew won't be holding most of the pieces.

***

A couple of hours turned into four and by then I was too tired to eat anything more than a bowl of cereal. I ate that, alone in my room, with my gaze trained to my phone.

I was tempted to reach out to Crew to ask when he'd be back, but he knows my number. If he felt the need to get in touch, he would have.

It's after two now, and I'm wide awake. I've opened the curtains and windows in my room to let the cool breeze and sounds of the night seep in. I thought that would help lull me back to sleep, but it hasn't.

I'm tempted to wander down the hallway that leads to the other wing of the house. I want to see if Crew is back. I didn't hear his car pull up but I didn't hear it when he took off hours ago either.

I watched him leave, without a glance back at me, wondering if I'd misjudged how easily either of us could go back to being just friends.

I swing my legs over the side of the bed and stand on the cool wood floor. I'm wearing white lace panties and a pink tank top. Normally, I sleep without a shirt, but I was fearful that I might have a nightmare and Crew would come bounding in my room to find me in tears and topless.

I pick up my phone from the nightstand and glance at the screen. The only messages are from

131

TROUBLEMAKER   *Deborah Bladon*

Sydney and Ellie from earlier this evening. Both asking if I'm having fun and, naturally, Ellie is worried that I forgot sunscreen. I ignored both messages when they first came in. I will until morning.

I walk to the window and look out but the darkness is infinite and unrelenting. I can't see beyond the edge of the wraparound deck. The small white lights that hang from the railing are swaying gently with the wind.

I move to the door, opening it slowly. I didn't bring a robe and my sweatpants are still on my bed back home, next to the shampoo and conditioner I planned on packing. As always, Crew had taken care of that. The bathroom that's attached to my bedroom here has everything I could need including the expensive Matiz hair products I rarely allow myself to buy.

I pad down the hallway toward the main room. I can tell the only light that is shining is the one I left on. It's on a small table next to the sofa by the fireplace. I thought if Crew came home, he'd need it to guide his way into the kitchen and beyond to his room.

I approach the front door and peek out through the glass that borders it. I can't see anything. No car, no Crew, just vast darkness beyond the lights that border the driveway.

A twisted knot settles in my stomach when I turn back around. There's no sign that Crew is here. His keys aren't on the foyer table where they normally are. My sandals are still right in the path of the doorway where I left them. He's tripped over them

TROUBLEMAKER   *Deborah Bladon*

twice since I got here which is why I keep putting them in the very same spot. He curses, I laugh and then he winks at me. That happened before this afternoon, before I shut him out as anything but my friend.

What if everything we had is now broken beyond repair?

Panic washes over me.

"Crew?" I call out into the empty house. "Crew. Please be here."

I wait to hear the sound of distant footsteps or his voice, but there's only dense silence surrounding me.

I close my eyes against the onslaught of conflicting emotions that hit me suddenly and violently.

I stumble toward the fireplace, my toes sweeping against the edge of the light gray area rug.

If he's not here that means he's still with the nameless woman he met for a drink hours ago.

He likes to drink, but even Crew wouldn't still be in a bar. He would have taken the party somewhere else.

I cover my face with my hands and kneel down, trying to stop the tears.

This is exactly what I wanted, but the pain is blinding. I pushed him away earlier to avoid this, but it's already too late. I'm in deeper than I've ever been before and this time I don't have a safety net. Before we kissed, I could convince myself it was for the best to stay at arm's length. I could make my heart shut up by dating other men. Now that I've tasted his mouth

133

TROUBLEMAKER   *Deborah Bladon*

and felt his hand on my skin, it's impossible to push aside what I feel.

I don't even know why I kissed him. I promised myself I wouldn't. I knew where this would go, but my strength was tattered that night. I was weak, too fragile to see the consequences clearly.

Now, he's with another woman, kissing her the way he kissed me. Touching her in the same way I've ached for.

I held a piece of his heart no one else ever has. I was his best friend until I wanted more. Now, it feels like I've lost that too.

I was fooling myself when I thought nothing would change. Everything is different.

I roll to my side, my body jerking with each sob I can't contain. Grief courses through me. I pushed away the only person who has always been there for me. He's my rock, the sole constant in my life that keeps me anchored.

He's the man who roared into my life like a heated summer night storm and saved me, even if he doesn't know it.

"Ad?" Crew's voice cracks through the still air. "Jesus, Adley."

I feel him before he's near me; the surge of feverish energy emanating from him is almost palpable. He's on his hands and knees before I can form a thought.

"Sweetheart." He pulls me into his big body from behind, his arms circling me. "Ad, please. You're scaring the fuck out of me. Tell me what's wrong."

TROUBLEMAKER   *Deborah Bladon*

I turn over quickly, burying my face in his bare chest. I cry every tear I've held in for the past five years as I cling to the man I can't live without.

Chapter 24

Crew

Time passes. Not quickly but at a snail's pace. I hold her tightly, wishing I could take her to my bed and keep her there, away from whatever or whoever caused this.

I got home hours ago, but she was already shuttered away in her room. I listened by the door, tempted to knock but there was no noise behind it. I took a walk outside around the property and looked in the direction of her bedroom. The curtains were drawn and the lights off so I ignored the urge to text her and I went to my room with a bottle of scotch.

I've seen her cry before but not like this.

This sliced me in two. I heard her call out as I went over projection numbers for the Matiz location in Phoenix. I took another sip of my drink to numb the pain I've been feeling since this afternoon when she told me that she needs me as a friend; just a friend, nothing more.

When I got out here she was on the floor. Broken.

"I've got you," I whisper again, for the third time.

I can't tell if my words are comforting or pissing her off. She hasn't responded. She hasn't moved. Her arms are wrapped around me, her head resting against my chest.

"Whatever it is, I can help." I can. Whatever the fuck happened, I can fix it.

TROUBLEMAKER   *Deborah Bladon*

Her legs move slightly, but she's as silent as she's been since I got on this cold, hard floor.

I press a kiss to the top of her head. "I'm going to pick you up. All you need to do is hold on."

"No," she whispers faintly. I barely hear it.

I'll stay on this fucking floor all night if what's what she wants, but I want her comfortable. "Let me put you on the sofa."

"I can get up," she hiccups out as her tears stop. "I can do it."

I know she can. She can do anything she puts her mind to, other than deal with whatever the fuck has gouged its way into her so deep that it's dragging her down.

I roll back and bounce to my feet, holding out a hand to help her.

She looks up, her face a swollen mess of despair. "I thought you were still out."

I nudge her up by her elbow, wrapping my arm around her waist. The skin on skin contact does my cock a favor. I'm dressed in pajama bottoms and nothing else. I can't mask what I'm feeling. I don't want to.

I might have agreed, in principle, to be the best friend forever, but that doesn't quiet my body's need for her.

She looks down at my obvious erection, straining against the soft black silk.

"I should go back to bed." Her eyes lock on mine. "Did I wake you?"

I shove both hands through my hair and exhale. I need to cool down. It suddenly feels hot as hell in here. "I was up."

TROUBLEMAKER   *Deborah Bladon*

"When did you get back?"

"Earlier," I offer without any explanation.

My reason for taking off this evening was simple. I needed air. Fresh air that didn't smell like her or taste like her. I couldn't look at her in that red bikini after I was friend-zoned.

I stood on that beach, with my eyes cast to the sand as she dipped her toes in the Atlantic for the first time. Then I returned the call of a woman I only see twice a year. When she proposed a drink, I suggested a place.

"What's eating you up?" I ask because she sure as hell isn't going to offer.

She keeps her emotions in a safe locked as tightly as my own.

"Nothing," she spits out the expected answer with a pout of her pink lips. "I had a bad dream."

"About what?" I push because I can smell bullshit a mile away and her response reeks.

She searches the air around us with her eyes for an answer. "I can't remember."

"What is eating you up?" I repeat my initial question. "Don't bullshit me, Adley."

She fidgets on her feet, her tits bouncing under the thin fabric of the tank top she has on. "I can't remember."

I inch forward, closing the space between us. "As we established, yet again this afternoon, we are friends. I'm the type of guy who doesn't like to see his friends all torn up, so if you want me to repeat the question again, I will and if you continue to offer me answers I don't believe, I'll keep asking."

138

TROUBLEMAKER   *Deborah Bladon*

Her hands lace together in front of her. "Maybe I was worried that you'd been in an accident. It's not like you drive all the time."

True, I don't, but when I do, I own the road. I step closer. "Try again."

She scowls. "Crew."

"Adley."

"What do you want me to say?" Her hands dart to her hips and those breasts, those sweet, round breasts of hers bounce yet again.

I'm not a tit man. I'm not a leg man either. A pretty cunt will make me hard as a bag of nails, but a perfect, heart shaped ass is what brings me to my knees.

With Adley, it's all of it. I want it all. I *still* want it all.

"Why were you so torn up?" I take that last step that separates us.

Her eyes travel over my chest, my biceps, my shoulders and then finally my face. I'm in no hurry. I'll wait all fucking night if she wants to take her time to visually inspect the goods.

"I'm going to bed," she says the words but she doesn't move an inch.

I do. I run the tip of my index finger over her forearm. "I'll go with you."

"What? Why?"

My finger travels up her shoulder before I bring it to her chin. "I want an answer to my question. Tell me what the hell happened before I walked in and found you on the floor."

Her bottom lip trembles just ever so slightly but she bites it to a halt. "You must be tired. You had

139

TROUBLEMAKER   *Deborah Bladon*

a long day. Why don't we just call it a night and talk about this in the morning?"

I cock both brows. "Because we're going to talk about it tonight."

Her hands move to her stomach. She inches up her shirt. It's a habit she has that she's completely unaware of it. She doesn't show much skin, but it's enough to tempt me yet again. "I need you to trust me to talk about this when I'm ready."

I grab her hand. I hold it against the warm skin of her stomach. "I want to help you."

She shudders. "You can't."

Like hell I can't.

"I have to figure this out on my own." Her hand grips mine tighter, sliding it up a quarter of an inch.

I stare down into her face. I want to kiss her. Fuck, do I want to kiss her.

"I'm here if you need me." I close my eyes because her skin is so soft and my dick isn't. I need another cold shower.

I had one when I got home and that had nothing to do with the woman I was with earlier. She wanted to introduce me to the friend she'd brought along to surprise me with. I wanted to come back here and stare at Adley.

The guy on the bar stool next to me hit the threesome lottery.

I hit the bitter edge of frustration when I got back and she was already fast asleep.

It felt like needles of ice were piercing my back as I stood in the shower, my cock in my palm,

140

TROUBLEMAKER   *Deborah Bladon*

while I thought about the petite blonde I'm looking at now.

"I'm going to bed," she announces like the inquisition has ground to a complete halt.

It has, for now.

With that she turns. I stand in silence watching the most perfect heart shaped ass covered in white lace, leave the room taking the most incredible woman in the world with it.

Chapter 25

Adley

Of course, he made me breakfast in bed. He's perfect.

"You didn't have to do this for me, Crew." I adjust the white blanket around my waist as I lean back on the cushioned headboard. "I could have come to have breakfast in the dining room."

"I waited half a fucking day for that." He rolls his mesmerizing green eyes. "It's almost noon, Ad."

"What?" I reach for my phone on the bedside table and scan the screen.

He's right.

I can't remember the last time I slept in this late. It has to be years. It was before...

"Can I place this tray down now?" He winks. "I swam laps in the pool for over an hour this morning and my arms are burnt."

I drum my fingers on my lap. "Put it here."

He places down a wooden breakfast tray covered in a linen napkin. There's coffee, orange juice, toast and a bowl of fresh berries. There's also a single rose. It's a lighter shade than the dozen that sit atop my bedside table but it's no less beautiful.

"This looks delicious." I look up at him.

He fingers the collar of the V neck gray T-shirt he's wearing. "Eat it all."

I nod sharply as I take a bite of the toast. "What time did you get up to swim?"

TROUBLEMAKER   *Deborah Bladon*

He walks backward before he lowers himself into a brown arm chair near the wall. "At five. I'm always up by five."

"Even on the weekends? Even out here?" I toss two blueberries into my mouth.

A sly smile crosses his lips. "Every day. I don't need much sleep."

Apparently not. I didn't get back into my room until close to three this morning which means he got to bed around the same time. Yet, he looks rested and ready to take on the day.

"Did you have fun last night?" I ask cautiously. It's a form of self-torture and the thoughts that kept my mind in motion until I finally gave in to the exhaustion and drifted off. I don't need or want details and yet I ask.

"Does it bother you that I met someone for a drink?"

I look over at where he's seated. His expression doesn't give anything away. He's not teasing which means it's a question he expects an answer to.

"It surprised me." I hold up my index finger. "Before you misunderstand what that means, I'll explain."

He tilts his chin down, but doesn't say anything.

"I get why you left." I curl my hand around the warm coffee mug. "You needed space. I think I did too. I guess I was just surprised that there was someone out here that you've seen before."

"We happened to be here, in the Hamptons, at the same time." He scratches the tip of his nose. "She

143

saw me at the market when I dropped by there on
Friday. She called me yesterday and the timing was
right."

"So it all worked out?" I inch up on the bed.
"You two had fun."

"She brought a friend along."

I bow my head. *A threesome.* It's not his first.

I hate the silence so I say the first thing that
comes to mind. "Double the fun. Lucky you."

His eyes eat into me as he swallows, his
Adam's apple bouncing in his neck. "Jealousy doesn't
look good on you."

"I'm not jealous."

In a heartbeat he's up from his chair and
sitting on the edge of the bed facing me. "A friend
can be jealous of a friend, Adley."

I look away. I don't want him this close to me,
not when he smells like Matiz cologne, raw lust and
all the bad decisions I'm dying to make. "I'm not
jealous," I repeat.

"Do I look like I had fun last night?"

I turn and gaze into his eyes. They're alight
with something. I feel it burning into me, igniting a
path straight to my core. "Yes."

A lazy smile runs over his lips. "The best part
of my night was laying on that hard as fuck floor with
you."

I feel my lips twitch. "That was the best part
of your night?"

He nods his head. "Nothing else came close."

I don't know how that makes sense. He
fucked two women, likely very beautiful women and

TROUBLEMAKER   *Deborah Bladon*

then got on the floor next to me while my hair was matted from being in a pool of my own tears.

"How's your heart today?" He looks at my shirt. Naturally, my nipples are at full attention.

"My heart?"

"I found some pieces of it on the floor this morning." He shoves his hand into the pocket of his blue shorts and then pulls it out with fanfare, showing me his empty palm. It's the same thing he does when he catches May crying. "Looks like you put it all back together yourself again. The way you always do."

He's right. I did, but it's not all there. He still has some pieces even if he can't see them.

***

"Jesus Christ, Adley," he says from behind me. "You get that any man, even a friend, is going to have a problem with you in that bikini."

"A problem?" I turn back to face him. "What's the problem?"

"It's too small."

It's not. It's actually perfect for me. It's white, a halter style top and a bottom that barely covers my ass.

I didn't put a lot of thought into my choice of swimwear when I was packing. I live in New York. If you go anywhere that warrants wearing a bikini, you bring every one you own.

After Crew took my breakfast tray away, I brushed my teeth and showered quickly. I chose this bikini because it was the first thing I grabbed out of my suitcase. I want to swim before the dark clouds

145

that are looming in the distance steal that chance away from me.

"I thought you said you had work to do," I ask because I'm genuinely curious.

He had said that when he left my room. He had to call a distributor about a facial cream. Beauty can't take a break, even on Sundays, it seems.

His lips twist wryly. "I'm very good at what I do. I handled that in twenty minutes flat."

I should probably bring up the fact that he told me earlier that it took him five hours yesterday to find a lost truck full of cosmetics, but I let it slide. "I'm going for a swim."

He glances at the pool behind me. "You know how to swim, right?"

I do. Swimming lessons were one of the afterschool activities my mom pushed on me when I was a kid. I'm grateful now, even though back then, I would have rather sat on my ass playing a video game than get in a pool with a bunch of strangers.

His phone rings again just as I'm about to tell him what a champion swimmer I think I am. He tugs it out of the pocket of his red board shorts. "Work. Fuck."

I don't bother asking whether he has to take it or not. I know he does. He always does.

"I'll hit the pool while you take care of business."

His thumb swipes the screen before he brings the phone to his ear spitting out his name as he answers.

I dive in the pool, letting the warm water steal away every ounce of tension in my body.

TROUBLEMAKER   *Deborah Bladon*

Chapter 26

Crew

I took the call, up at the house and then I jerked off.

A man can only take so much off-limits ass and tits in his face before he has to do something to relieve the pressure.

I watched her swim while I was talking to my brother-in-law, Ryker, about a meeting he's taking tomorrow. He's married to my sister, the father of my nephew and my right hand man at Matiz. He handles marketing and many of the small fires that erupt.

Giving him some extra work to handle this weekend seemed like a great idea until my sister chewed me out in a text message.

Ryker, like Nolan, devotes his weekends to his family. I devote it to managing whatever needs my attention at Matiz and my clubs.

What needs my attention right now is Adley.

She swam like the goddess she is in the water, her fleshy ass bobbing up and down as she lapped the length of the pool seven times before she got out.

That in itself brought my cock to its brink. Curves, beads of water and wet hair all added to my stable of fantasy images of her.

That's when my hand found my dick and I jacked off in front of the bedroom window, while I watched her towel off her perfect body.

She's still down near the pool, even though the approaching clouds promise an impressive show of

147

TROUBLEMAKER   *Deborah Bladon*

lightning and angry thunder. It's barreling down on us fast.

I grab a bottle of water from the fridge in the kitchen before I'm out the door and on my way toward her.

My phone rings, again. I tug it out of my pocket then silence it immediately.

This time the caller can wait.

"You're finally done," Ad calls as I approach, a bright smile covering her mouth. She's on a lounger, in a half-reclining position. Her hand is over her head, the other on her stomach. It's a reminder of how I found her on my sofa.

I crack open the water and push it at her. "Are you ready to come back up to the house?"

She takes the bottle and downs a large swallow, her neck working to handle it all.

I may have come within the last twenty minutes but I could go again for her.

"I'm going to wait until the rain starts."

I sit on the lounger next to her, facing her so I can soak in the image of her body. Our *just friends* agreement needs to be brought back to the table for renegotiation since it's clearly not working for me.

I turned down a threesome last night and I instantly deleted a text message Lucia sent me two hours ago with a short video attached.

It was likely porn site quality since every video she's ever sent me of her getting herself off has been. My cock wasn't interested so I deleted it before I even read the message.

My wet dream is currently licking water from her lips with her eyes closed.

148

TROUBLEMAKER   *Deborah Bladon*

Her hand snakes lower on her stomach so it skims the edge of those tiny white bikini bottoms.

I want to reach out and trail my fingers behind hers until they dive under the fabric.

If I can't have that, I want to watch her get herself off.

"Did you see me at the window?" I ask because she did look to the house briefly, but her eyes skimmed the exterior before they dropped back down.

"No." She looks at me. Her hand is traveling up her stomach now in a slow circular pattern. "Were you watching to make sure I didn't drown?"

My eyes are glued to her fingers. They inch up closer to her left breast. Her nipples are as hard now as they were when I kissed her. I want to slice my teeth over one until she yelps again.

"Not exactly," I answer cautiously.

Her hand is on the move again, faster now, tracing circles around her bellybutton. Her eyelids flutter shut, her breathing shallow. "What were you doing?"

I reach out because fuck if I'm going to be able to control this. I just want a touch. My hand lands on top of hers.

Her eyes fly open, her lips quiver, but not a sound leaves them.

She doesn't say *no*, there isn't a *yes*, but it's understood that she welcomes the touch. The shift of her thighs as they rub together tells me as much.

"I was watching you," I say before a loud clap of thunder makes her flinch.

I clasp my hand over hers, still pressing it against her navel.

149

She doesn't say anything so I take the lead, because fuck if I am going to give up this easily when it comes to her.

"You're too beautiful not to look at." I rake her body from head-to-toe, slowly, savoring every inch of her flawless skin.

Her hand creeps lower, taking mine with it.

"Am as I as beautiful as the two women you were with last night?"

I stare at our hands, the fingers linked together as they slide over her skin. "I didn't fuck them and no, neither of them compares to you."

"You didn't?" she asks like she expects that I can drive my dick into anyone but her. I'm beginning to wonder if I'll ever be able to again without having to close my eyes to imagine it's her beneath me.

"I didn't want to."

She edges our fingers lower until I feel the graze of the soft fabric of those tiny bikini bottoms against my fingertips. "Why?"

If she wants me to answer honestly, I will. Fuck the consequences because I'm in so deep that I'm drowning in lust. "They weren't you."

"Crew," she purrs as our fingers pass over the triangle of fabric that separates her cunt from my touch. "We agreed to be…"

"Friends." I finish for her. "I know. Believe me I fucking know but that isn't going to extinguish the want, Ad. You're gorgeous."

Her breathing quickens as she takes my hand on a journey along her inner thigh. "It would change things."

TROUBLEMAKER   *Deborah Bladon*

I exhale when our fingers skim her cleft over the fabric before she glides them over her other thigh. "That would depend on what we do. We handled the kiss, we can handle more."

"How much more?" Her eyes lock on mine. They're filled with the same crushing need I feel inside of me.

"You decide." I tilt my chin to where our hands are circling her thigh, so goddamn close to what I want to touch. My cock wants in too, but I bite back the urge to pull it out and fist it.

She holds my gaze as she glides our linked hands to the top of the bikini bottoms, before she dips them inside.

Chapter 27

Adley

Our hands stop, his knuckles grazing the smooth skin under my bikini bottoms.

"You want this?" His words are laced with desire so thick that I can almost taste it on my tongue. I want to kiss his mouth but he's still sitting on the lounger next to me, his cock swollen under his shorts.

I nod because I don't want to hear myself say how much I want his hands on my skin, or his mouth or his cock inside of me, anywhere he'll put it.

He pushes my fingers along the seam of my pussy. I'm so wet. I've never been this wet before.

"Jesus," he hisses out between clenched teeth. "You're soft and so fucking wet."

I inch his fingers forward, wanting him to touch me the way I always touch myself when I think about him.

"Show me how you like it," he whispers as if the clouds and wind can hear us.

I dip a finger between my folds, honing in on that swollen nub of nerves. I'm tempted to circle it myself, so I can get off before he gets his hand on it. I know I won't last when that happens. It already feels like my core is on fire.

"Your cunt feels beautiful."

I moan from that because I knew, I just knew, that when I heard him say it, that I'd fall apart inside.

TROUBLEMAKER   *Deborah Bladon*

"Such sweet little sounds." He looks at my face before his gaze drops back to where our hands are still linked together, hidden from our view.

I pull my fingers from his, slowly, wanting nothing between his touch and my arousal.

"I'll take it from here." He smiles a devilish grin that tells me that he's going to make me feel things I've never felt before.

I slide my hand back and cry out as soon as his fingers touch my folds.

My legs fall open because I want more. My arm jumps up to shield my face. I won't let him see how badly I want this, how badly I've always wanted it.

"Let me see you." His free hand grabs my wrist and twists my arm away. "I want to see you come undone."

I bite my lip when he slides his finger from my pussy. I almost protest until I feel his thumb on my clit.

I bow my back because the pleasure is too much. It's a light touch that should only set me on the path to a buzz, but it's more than that. It's electric and raw, sending bursts of tender need to every cell of my body.

"I knew you'd feel this good." His eyes darken as he stares at my face. "Do you know how much I've wanted to touch this? How much I think about it?"

It can't be as much as I do.

He slides a finger back inside me and I groan from the pure need to get off.

Thunder claps an uneven concert above our heads as the first drops of rain pepper our skin.

153

TROUBLEMAKER   *Deborah Bladon*

"I want to savor this." He gestures to where his hand is working slowly, painfully slowly, on my pussy under the white fabric. "But the storm is coming."

I look down, dizzy from the image of his hidden fingers; their intent clear.

"I'll take it from you quickly this time."

This time.

He knows as well as I do that we're crossing a line in the sand that will be forever lost to the waves. We can't go back from this. I don't want to anymore.

I cry out when he slides another thick finger in me. I stomp my foot when he circles my clit so painfully gently that I can feel the edge of the cliff. Then when he hones in on that spot inside of me, I let go. I pulse around his fingers when the orgasm rips through me.

He groans out my name as I cling to the edge of the past and the unknown of the future.

***

"Ad?" His voice carries through the sound of the thunder. "You're so fucking beautiful like this."

I open my eyes. He's on his knees next to me, his breath racing a hot path over the skin of my stomach.

The rain is coming down harder now, heavy pebbles against our skin.

His hand is still in my bikini bottoms. His fingers still moving slowly over my tender flesh, making me ache for even more.

TROUBLEMAKER   *Deborah Bladon*

"We did that," I whisper into the palm of my hand. "We did it."

"We did." He leans forward and kisses the back of my fingers. "We'll do it again as soon as you let me take you up to the house."

I close my eyes against the now steady rain that is saturating us both.

I feel alive in a way I've never felt before. My entire body is tingling. My pulse is racing and I can't fathom how I'm going to stand after what just happened.

I shift my legs. "I should get up."

He clenches his hand over my pussy, and I grit my teeth.

Jesus.

Pleasure pulses through my body again. I could come just from the look in his eyes and those fingers kneading the lips of my sex.

"I want you in my bed when we get up to the house."

There's no charm in his words. He's not trying to seduce me. He knows I'm willing to follow him like a stray puppy looking for its next meal.

His touch is more addictive than I imagined it would be.

"We should talk." My own words bite into me, waves of confusion crash inside of me.

I should just take the plunge and race him to his bed. My common sense needs to shut up and let me feel. I want to feel again. I want it to be with him.

He hovers above me, his fingers finally easing out of my bikini.

155

"If that's what you need, that's what we'll do." His lips feather a trail of soft kisses over my forehead. "Let's get you out of the rain."

He offers his hand and I take it, letting him help me to my feet. I look down at my bikini. It's soaked from the rain and from his touch.

As he leads me to the house, the storm picks up intensity. The wind whips around at a pace as brisk as the hammering of my heart.

Chapter 28

Crew

I light a fire because the storm has stolen the warmth out of the air. I also do it to kill time. Adley told me she wanted to rinse the chlorine from the pool of off her body an hour ago, so she went into her room to shower. I didn't follow her although I wanted nothing more.

A shower wasn't what I needed. I'm not washing away the sweet smell of her from my hand anytime soon. What happened earlier was an appetizer. It was a sample of what awaits me.

I hear her gentle footsteps on the hardwood floor before I see her round the corner.

She's wearing a thin white dress that is almost sheer. I can tell immediately that she's not wearing a bra and that her panties are white too.

"Hi," she says when she nears.

I don't want her to feel anything but completely comfortable around me. She cast her head down when we ran from the rain. Once we were inside, she was down the hall so quickly that I couldn't say a thing in response to her announcement that she was having a shower.

"Sit with me." I pat the spot next to me on the sofa.

Her eyes skim over my clothes. Black T-shirt, matching sweatpants and nothing else.

"Do you want some wine? A soda?" I fist my hand on my thigh to prevent myself from reaching out

TROUBLEMAKER   *Deborah Bladon*

to touch her knee once she's settled beside me. "I can get you anything you want."

Her gaze lands on my lips. "I'm fine. Thank you."

"You're scared," I say it because I see it. It's there, not only in her face but in her body language too. Her shoulders are tense. Her hands folded tightly in her lap.

She nods as she bows her head. "I don't think you understand how much I need a friend like you."

I get it. I need her too. I have other friends, some women, but none are as close to me as she is. She's the person I depend on to give it to me straight. She's also one of the few people in this world who doesn't give two shits that I'm rich or successful.

Ad likes me for me, and in my world, that's a rarity.

"I understand," I offer gently. "I need you just as much as you need me."

Her head pops up. "I don't think so, Crew. You have a lot of friends. Probably ten times as many as I do. If things happened that would pull us apart, you'd have someone else to go to. There's always a friend a call away for you."

It's true, but those friendships are shallow at best. They can't compare to what the two of us share.

"I have very few close friends."

A smile curves her lip, but it's gone with the next beat of my heart. "I know I'm one of the close ones. I think I know you better than most of your friends."

158

TROUBLEMAKER   *Deborah Bladon*

There's something woven into the words. They hold a weight to them beyond the obvious. "You do know a lot about me."

"And then some," she adds in a whisper.

My heart drums against the wall of my chest in strong, measured beats. There are things I've never told her about me. Things I've only told Nolan and I would bet my life and hers that he would never break that confidence. "What do you know about me?"

Her gaze roams my face. "You're a good friend."

"I'm an even better lover," I quip.

She rubs her hands on her thighs. "What if it all goes to hell? How will we handle that?"

I don't see that as an option so devising a plan is a waste of my time. I want her, and that goes beyond the sex. I want her heart. I want it all because I'm seeing her in a way I haven't before.

"What if it doesn't go to hell?"

She sits back. "You like women too much for this to not go to hell at some point."

It stings. Her words cut through me with the force of a jagged knife because it's my actions that have given her those thoughts and those words. We may not talk about who we're fucking but there are enough clues in my life that I'm getting my fair share of pussy for her to know what's going on.

Condom packages in the guest room nightstand because sometimes I want to fuck with a different view of the city.

Panties strung around the hanger when I pick up my suits from the dry cleaners after they fished them out of my pockets.

159

TROUBLEMAKER   *Deborah Bladon*

Lipstick tubes nestled between the cushions of my leather couch.

The list goes on…

Adley has seen all of that and more.

"I haven't fucked a woman since I kissed you."

Her brow furrows as she considers those words. "You haven't?"

"I don't want to," I admit on a heavy exhale. "I want you, Adley."

"Why now?" Her hands twist together in a knot of anxiety. I want to reach out and grab them, cradle them against my chest so she can feel my heart beat for only her.

I straighten slowly. "It's not a new thing. It's been building for months."

"It has?" Her voice jumps an octave with the question. "Since when?"

I shrug. "New Year's Eve? Maybe even before."

She thinks about it before she responds. "Why didn't you say something then?"

It's an honest question that I don't have a straightforward answer to. "I knew you'd push me back on it. I know how much you value our friendship."

"I thought you did too." Her response is quick and harsh. "I thought you understood that our friendship is an essential part of my life. I'm scared to lose that. I can't describe how fucking scared I am by that, Crew."

I am too. I admit I'm feeling things for her that I've never felt before but I have no fucking clue

160

TROUBLEMAKER   *Deborah Bladon*

where they'll take us. All I know is that I'm willing to hang on for the ride.

"We'll take it as slowly as you want." I reach over and finally grab her hand. "Are you feeling all right about what we did by the pool?"

She laces her fingers together with mine. "I am."

I take that as a win. "I am too."

Her brows shoot up as she smiles. "I thought you would be."

"I want more." I tilt my chin down and gently squeeze her hand. "I want to taste every inch of you. I want to be inside of you."

Her breathing stutters. I know that if I slid my fingers into her panties, she'd be ready for me; warm and wet, just as she was by the pool. "Slowly, right?"

I inch closer to her, wanting to taste her sweet lips. "I like it slow, Ad."

She nods. "I like it slow too."

I breathe in the scent of the skin of her neck. Long, pulling intakes of air that smell of her perfume and beneath that, her. It's fresh, sensuous and baits me to kiss her under her ear.

"I touched your cunt. I want to taste it."

She shivers under those words. Her head falls back against the couch. "Your mouth does things to me."

"You have no idea what it can do to you." I inch the hem of her dress up with my hand. "Let me show you."

She turns her head toward me, pressing her lips to mine. I trail my hand up her thigh as I slide my

161

tongue along hers; devouring her mouth the same way I'll devour her pussy.

I fuck her mouth, my tongue taking from hers. My teeth scraping her bottom lip as a warning, and a dark promise of what it will feel like once my head is between her legs and her clit between my teeth.

She moans into the kiss, her hand reaching up to weave between the strands of my hair.

I tap the silk of her panties feeling how wet they already are.

I pull back from the kiss but only far enough to speak. "I want you on my bed, naked so I can taste all of this."

I squeeze her through her panties and that alone is enough to raise her ass from the sofa. I press soft circles over her clit using the rough friction of the fabric to tempt her.

"You know how to use your hands," she pants. "How the hell are you so good with your hands?"

Years of unnecessary experience.

It's always been the quickest way to get a woman worked up enough that my cock could slide in without any resistance.

"Wait until you meet my tongue." I smile against her cheek. "My cock is dying to meet you too."

Her hips circle as she chases an orgasm. "I feel like I could come right here on the spot."

"Do it," I hiss the words out as I rim the shell of her ear with my tongue. "Or I can drop to my knees and lick that beautiful cunt."

"Please," she fists my hair in her hand. "Oh, God, yes please."

TROUBLEMAKER   *Deborah Bladon*

I stand and yank my T-shirt over my head. I tug on the drawstring of my sweatpants because if I'm going down on her, I'm going to need something in return once I've given her an orgasm or three.

I start to slide them down as her eyes lock on the thin trail of dark hair that disappears under the waistband.

A loud rustling by the front door twists my head in that direction.

Adley's on her feet, her hands pinned to my back, her head peeking out from behind my bicep as the door opens and my brother walks in with a brunette on his arm.

"Hey, Crew," Kade calls from the doorway as he drops two overnight bags on the floor. "You don't mind if we crash your little party, do you?"

I stare at the woman standing next to my younger brother.

Fuck her. Fuck my life.

"You didn't mention your brother would be here, Kade," she drawls through her red lips. "It's good to see you, Crew. I haven't seen you since you left me at the altar."

Chapter 29

Adley

Altar? He left a woman at the altar? How is it that he's never told me he was engaged?

I watch in silence as the beautiful woman approaches us. Her hair is black with caramel highlights. It's cut into a stylish bob that showcases the perfect bone structure of her face.

Her eyes are a deep brown and framed by lashes that most women would kill for.

"Who is this?"

She looks at me like I should be shining her shoes.

"I'm Adley," I pipe up and extend a hand because Crew is as frozen as a statue.

"It's good to meet you, Ashley." She takes my hand and wipes her fingertips across my palm. I have no idea if that's a supermodel handshake or what but I'm grateful for the minimal touching.

"Her name is Adley," Kade corrects her with a smile. He looks every part the Hampton weekender with his jeans, blue polo shirt and expensive haircut. The last time I saw him, his brown hair was cropped short. Now it's longer on top, giving him a look that suits him better.

"I'm Damaris."

It's a beautiful name for a striking woman.

"Why are you here?" Crew directs the question at his brother as he tugs his T-shirt back over his head. "Why the hell would you bring her?"

164

TROUBLEMAKER   *Deborah Bladon*

"We're friends," Kade answers quickly, his gray eyes scanning Crew's face. "You know that we're friends, Crew."

"Did you know that I was up here with Adley?"

I can answer that question. When Kade texted me three days ago to see how things were going, I mentioned my weekend trip. I didn't tell him that I was headed here with Crew, but he apparently connected those dots on his own.

"Adley told me, but I thought you'd be gone by now." He taps the face of his wristwatch. "Isn't it dinner with your friends on Sunday night, then you at your desk first on Monday morning? You're running behind schedule."

"I'm here until tomorrow night." He crosses his arms over his chest.

"Fair enough." Kade moves to stand next to Crew's ex-fiancée. "Damaris needed a break from the city. I needed a day off work, so we're here for the night."

"You're leaving." Crew widens his stance.

"I'll take my old room." Kade turns to talk to Damaris. "You'll bunk in Lark's old room. Does that work for you, Crew?"

"No."

"Why not?"

"You need to leave now, Kade." He gestures toward the front door. "Get lost."

"If you can bring a friend up here, I sure as hell can too." Kade squeezes my bicep. "I'm not going anywhere."

TROUBLEMAKER   *Deborah Bladon*

"Fuck it. Then we are." Crew turns to his side to look down at me. "Pack up your stuff. We're leaving."

I've never seen him this on edge before. Usually, when he gets angry, it's always laced with humor. He's a master at controlling his temper, but that's not the person I see in front of me now.

"Crew?" I reach for his forearm, but he brushes my hand away.

"Get ready to go, Ad." His eyes dart between Damaris and me. "Now."

I nod.

Crew's on his way to the kitchen and the bedrooms beyond before I've taken a step. I fold my arms over my chest, suddenly aware that my dress is sheer.

"I'm sorry, Adley." Kade wraps his arm around my shoulder. "I didn't mean to fuck up your entire weekend."

I'm sorry too. Not only did Crew and I get interrupted at the worst possible time, but I met his ex-fiancée; a woman I didn't know existed until now.

"It's fine," I lie. "I need to get back to the real world anyway."

"You're from New York too, yes?" Damaris moves to look at me. "You and Crew are friends?"

"She's one of his best friends," Kade offers. "She keeps him in line."

I smile at him. In the text I sent him about my trip, I didn't mention anything about the kiss. It's not his business. It's a secret that only Crew and I share.

"I used to keep him in line." Damaris laughs. "We were friends too, but then it was more."

166

TROUBLEMAKER   *Deborah Bladon*

"And then he made a mistake and let you go," Kade adds.

"You would have been the best brother-in-law." She turns from Kade to study my face. "Have we met before?"

"No," I answer quickly because if I met this woman I sure as hell would remember it. She could jump on any catwalk and strut herself to a million dollar contract.

"Your face is so familiar to me." Her finger darts to her chin. "Maybe we've seen each other in the city. What do you do for work?"

"That's none of your business," Crew says from where he's standing to our left. He has his gray pants on and his hands are making quick work of the buttons of his black shirt.

"I'll get ready to go." I glance at Damaris one more time. I should be polite and tell her that it's nice to meet her, but that's a lie.

"He needs a friend." She jerks her thumb at Crew. "I'm glad he has a good one in you."

He has something in me. I'm not sure what it is anymore.

***

Once we're on the highway, I ask the question that has been perched on my lips since Damaris walked into the foyer with Kade. "When were you two together?"

"That altar stuff is bullshit." He doesn't look at me. His eyes stay on the road as he handles his BMW

TROUBLEMAKER   *Deborah Bladon*

with ease. "I broke off our engagement in person before we'd even picked a date. It was brief, Ad."

"It was before we met," I say that aloud even though I don't mean to.

"Years before." He nods his head. "We were only together for a few months."

I stare out the window at the traffic passing on the other side of the highway. "Where did you meet?"

He hesitates before he answers. His jaw tightens as his hands fist the steering wheel. "At a club. I always met women at clubs."

We met outside a club in Vegas. It's not the same though. He didn't even acknowledge me that night. He was focused on Ellie because he wanted to offer her a job, and then on Lucia because he wanted to offer her his cock.

"You loved her." I push my hands against my thighs. I changed into jeans and a white sweater. They were the first items I grabbed as I heard Crew's shoe tapping on the floor outside the door of the bedroom.

"No." He briefly looks at me before his eyes are on the road again. "I liked what we did together. I liked the high she provided. That's not love."

"Have you ever been in love?" I ask because maybe his gauge is different than mine. I don't know what love feels like to anyone but me.

"No," he answers quickly. "I love people, but that's not the same."

He's right. It's not.

He clears his throat. "You loved Leo."

My head darts in his direction. I feel a sense of panic hearing him say Leo's name. I've spoken to him about my ex-boyfriend before, but that was right

TROUBLEMAKER   *Deborah Bladon*

after Crew and I met. I was still hung up on Leo because he had helped me heal after the end of a relationship that damaged me in countless ways.

I missed Leo's presence in my life for months after our split. I didn't miss the arguments we constantly had over our undecided mutual future.

Leo wanted to get married and have a child right away. I want a career and the chance to grow into the person I'm supposed to be before I hold my own baby in my arms.

"I did love him," I admit on a sigh. "It wasn't a good fit for me though. If it were, I wouldn't have fallen out of love with him so easily."

He reaches for my hand and brings it to his thigh. "Leo was a lucky man."

Damaris was a lucky woman. She got him to drop to his knee and offer his life to her. Knowing Crew the way I do, that's a shock.

"Do you ever regret ending it?" I try to pull my hand back but he holds it tightly.

"Never."

I look back out the window and the darkening sky. "I take it you two don't talk anymore."

He lets my hand slip away when I give it another tug. "There's nothing left for us to talk about. She was part of my life, now she's not. It's cut and dry."

I fall silent as we make a turn.

He loved her enough to ask her to marry him once.

They started as friends and ended like this. I don't want that to be our story too.

169

Chapter 30

Crew

I have no idea what was running through Adley's mind when I dropped her off at her apartment last night. I helped her carry her bags up to her door, and when Sydney opened it to pull Adley into a tight hug, any chance we had to say goodbye was lost.

She didn't turn back to say anything to me after she thanked me for the weekend.

I went home, stood in my shower for over thirty minutes and then drank myself to sleep.

"You're back a day early." Nolan waltzes into my office with a spring in his step. It's been there since he asked Ellie to marry him. "I rearranged a half dozen of your meetings. That was a waste of my fucking time."

The grin on his face tells me he's joking. Even if he weren't, I wouldn't give a shit. I've helped him build this company into what it is today. He's rewarded me handsomely for that in the form of a corner office and a percentage of shares.

I may not own as much stock in Matiz Cosmetics as he does, but I work for our success harder than he ever has.

It started as a friend helping a friend after he inherited the business. It turned into much more when I rode the adrenaline high to our first million. Now, our yearly sales are more than either of us could have imagined.

TROUBLEMAKER   *Deborah Bladon*

It affords us both a comfortable life, so you'll hear no complainants about the investment in time and effort it took to get us here.

"Kade showed up in Westhampton Beach. He wasn't alone."

Nolan's mouth twitches as he takes a seat in one of the chairs in front of my desk. "Who was with him?"

"You're going to flip your shit. I couldn't believe my eyes when she walked through the door."

"Jesus, don't tell me it was Damaris."

I cock a brow.

"What a stupid little fuck." He rubs his hand over his chin. "Your brother is an asshole. Have you noticed that?"

I huff out a deep laugh. "His story is that he thought Adley and I were on our way back to the city. He brought Damaris up there for a recharge."

"Why the fuck has he stayed friends with her?" Both his hands run through his brown hair. "I get that they were friends before you two got together, but still."

I have no clue why they're friends. They went to college together but their connection didn't lead to our meeting. "Who the fuck knows? That's not the point. The point is that he brought her up to the house when I was supposed to be alone with Ad."

"How did she react to meeting your ex?"

I've only thrown Nolan bare scraps of information about Ad and me. She's his wife's best friend so he can't keep his mouth shut about Adley if he knows something Ellie doesn't. "It was awkward for everyone, pal."

171

TROUBLEMAKER   *Deborah Bladon*

"Other than the crazy ex showing up, how did the weekend go?"

"It was good," I say on a heavy breath. "We're closer than we were when we left. I think we're in a better place."

Or we were until Damaris showed up.

"Good to hear." He doesn't press for more, and I'm thankful for that.

"I'll take over the eleven o'clock and the two o'clock meetings with marketing." I tap the end of a pen on a folder on my desk. "You're off the hook."

"Taking an extra day to fuck around your apartment wouldn't have killed you." Nolan stands and buttons his suit jacket. "We don't need your ass in here every single day."

They do. He chooses to believe otherwise.

"Look, I'm only asking this because I'm worried about you. Did Damaris say anything about the …"

I stop him before the word leaves his lips. That word. My personal hell is bundled up in one word that forever changed my life. Damaris was there for me on the worst day of my life. Every day after that, she chose to remind me of the pain I was in. It was her weapon to make me weak.

"She didn't," I cut him off. "She kept her mouth shut."

"Maybe she does have a heart after all." He looks over my shoulder at the open door of my office. He knows my assistant is on her break or this conversation wouldn't be happening.

She doesn't. Damaris has a big bank account, thanks to my generosity when we split. She wanted

172

TROUBLEMAKER   *Deborah Bladon*

the wedding of her dreams. I wanted my freedom. We both got exactly what we needed.

***

I slow as I near her. She's outside her apartment, white pants and a navy blouse covering her body. She's wearing nude heels and a pair of sunglasses.

"Adley," I call out to her as she raises her hand to flag down a taxi. "Wait up."

She slides the sunglasses onto her head, as her eyes skim me from head-to-toe. "You're wearing a suit. Did you go to the office today?"

Work is my drug of choice. When I'm sitting in my office at the top of the Matiz tower, I feel centered. I needed that today after seeing Damaris in the Hamptons.

"I had some work to catch up on." It's not a complete lie. There is always something to do in my world, whether it's managing the concerns of a Matiz employee or signing off on a shipment of vodka at the club.

"I'm going to see a friend."

I follow her gaze when it drops to her phone and a text message appears. She covers it with her other hand before I can read anything beyond "*Hi Adley.*"

"What friend?" I ask because she's always been an open book. She's never gotten on me for invading her space even though she's never invaded mine.

173

"You don't know them."

Them. Not her, not him, but them. It's a man.

"What's his name?" I don't even try and mask the heaviness of my tone.

Her eyes dart over my face. "Don't act like a caveman, Crew. I have other friends."

I know she does. Most of them are women.

"Is it someone I know?" I press for more like a sixteen-year-old kid who is worried his steady is going to kiss the star quarterback behind the bleachers.

"No."

I stare at her because that's not a satisfactory answer. "Who is it, Ad?"

"His name is John." She takes a step around me toward the curb. "Are you happy now?"

Fuck no, I'm not. She's never mentioned a man named John to me so this is coming straight out of left field.

"Where did you meet?" I keep my tone calm as I watch her wave her arm in the air as an already occupied taxi approaches.

She stomps her foot when it flies by.

"That one wasn't available." I look down at my phone and thumb out a message.

"I knew that. What are you doing here anyway?"

"I'm here to take you to dinner." I pocket my phone again. "I want to talk about the weekend."

"It's over." She squints as another occupied taxi whizzes past us.

Panic bubbles in my chest, seeping into my lungs. I exhale and try to draw in a deep breath.

TROUBLEMAKER   *Deborah Bladon*

"The weekend is over, not us." She turns to look at me. "I was surprised by the fact that you were engaged once. You. Engaged. Who would have thought?"

"She means nothing to me now, Adley."

Her hand jumps to my arm. "I know and I'm glad, but a part of me is freaking out about that."

"Why?" I grab her wrist and pin her hand to my cheek. "Why are you freaking out over the fact that I dumped Damaris?"

She opens her palm and cradles my face. I close my eyes because the touch is almost too much. I've been starving for her all day and this small morsel of her attention isn't enough to satiate the hunger.

"You were friends once, you fucked, fell in love and then you broke up."

I get it. She's terrified that we're going to travel down that same road. What she doesn't understand is that what I felt for Damaris was a dim light compared to the blinding sunshine that surrounds me whenever she's near me. "I never cared about her the way I care about you."

"We'll figure this out." She brushes her fingertips over my cheek. "We'll take this slowly and if it feels like too much for either of us, we stop, we talk and we decide together whether it's still the right thing."

"Agreed," I say because I can't tell her that it's never going to feel like it's too much. She's not ready to hear that yet.

"Is that Bill?" She points at a black SUV coming up the street.

TROUBLEMAKER   *Deborah Bladon*

"He's right on time." I smile as he approaches. "I just sent him a text. He's going to take you where you need to go."

The car pulls up on the street next to us. She waves to Bill before she turns back to me. "You know I could have gone to see John without your help."

John, fucking John.

"Tell John to keep his dick in his pants."

Her eyes lock on my mouth before they drift to my eyes. "He's twice my age. It's not like that."

"Tell me what it's like." I step closer to her and rest my hands on her shoulders.

"I'm not ready to." The fingers on her left hand tap dance over the front of her neck. "When I'm ready to talk about it, you'll be the first person I tell."

It stings. It fucking stings but a secret isn't just hers to hold. I have my own share that I've kept hidden from her for the past two years.

"I'll call you tonight," I say before I press my lips to her forehead.

She looks up at me. "You're still the best friend I've ever had."

I know it. I'm also the man who is falling in love with her.

176

Chapter 31

Adley

I watch Crew when I walk in the club. He has two favorite spots. The first is up on the VIP level. He stands there, usually dressed all in black, with a glass of something amber in his hand and a woman next to him. He'll kiss her before his hand inches down her back.

I always know the exact moment when his fingers reach their final destination. Her mouth will curve into an 'O,' her head will rock back onto his chest, and she'll start to move her hips in small circles.

To anyone else, it looks like they're dancing. His hand will be in the air balancing the glass and her hands will grip tightly to the metal railing in front of her. She'll close her eyes and move slowly.

As the tempo of the music increases, so do her movements.

Depending on how she likes it, she'll push her legs further apart to give him more of what he wants.

He'll take a drink, she'll bite her lips and then she'll shudder. Sometimes violently, other times subtly, but I always know when she comes on his hand. It doesn't matter who she is. The telltale signs are there.

His other perch is at the end of the bar.

That's where he is now. Surveying his club, watching its patrons, hunting for something.

I've seen him take countless women up to the VIP area from the dance floor, sometimes one, often two.

Waiting for them to come back down isn't usually part of my plan. It happens though. The elevator always arrives first with the woman or women he's spent an hour or two with.

Then he'll ride it back down, a look of smug satisfaction on his face, and the scent of sex peppering his skin as he walks past where I'm standing near the bar, oblivious to the fact that I've been at the club many nights when he has too.

I didn't go to seek him out. My drinks were free so when friends from work wanted a place to let loose, I'd invite them to the club for a round on me. I'd dance, have fun, talk to men and unwind.

More often than not, Crew wouldn't be there, but when he was, he'd never notice I was there. I never approached because I knew what he was there for and it had nothing to do with me.

"You should go say hello to your dreamboat." Sydney taps me on the shoulder. "He looks lonely."

He looks ready to pounce on a brunette in a short pink dress who is bouncing to the beat of a song I've had on repeat for days. I make a mental note to delete it from my phone.

"I'm going to hang back," I say as I watch Crew stand. "Go have fun."

She's off on a dash toward a group at the opposite end of the bar. I haven't taken my eyes off Crew since he walked in. His eyes haven't left his target.

TROUBLEMAKER   *Deborah Bladon*

Brunette, small tits, cute ass, and a smile that could light up the darkest night.

He told me he'd call tonight. He will, but I knew he'd likely be here so after my meeting I went home, changed and shared an Uber with Sydney. She was headed here to meet her friends, and I tagged along knowing I'd find him in one of his two favorite spots.

He's always here on Monday nights, and most other nights too.

I watch from the shadows as he circles the woman, not once, but twice.

It's a scene I've witnessed at least a dozen times but never before has my heart thundered in my ears like this. It's almost deafening, drowning out the music along with all rational thought.

I shouldn't do this. I should walk up to him so he knows I'm here, but my memory is clouded with so many images like the one happening right before my eyes, that I don't move.

My breath catches when he takes a step closer to her. Her eyes meet his. She turns so she's facing him directly.

Crew holds out his hand and I almost fall to my knees. My stomach recoils and I'm afraid that the salad I had for dinner will end up all over my little black dress.

She reaches for his touch because there's no reason for her not to. He's gorgeous, imposing and it's obvious that the man knows how to fuck. That energy seeps from every single pore of his body.

He pulls her closer and then he drops her hand and his arms cross over his chest.

TROUBLEMAKER   *Deborah Bladon*

Another man approaches, dressed in all black too. He's security. I know that. He takes a place next to Crew. They talk, to each other and then the woman and she glances around the room, her eyes darting helplessly in despair. She's searching for something or someone.

She pivots on her pink heels but the security officer has his hand on her elbow. She tries to shake him off, tears well in the corner of her eyes and then her head drops.

That's when he turns. Crew turns in my direction and across the dimly lit space, through the crowds that filter past me on their way into and out of the club, he locks his eyes on mine and a brilliant smile takes over his beautiful mouth.

***

"I don't know what the fuck is wrong with these kids who try to worm their way into the club." He shakes his head as the woman in the pink dress is guided toward the exit by the security guard. "It doesn't take a fucking genius to see that she's underage. I swear the people who work the door all need to have their asses kicked."

He smiles through that rant.

"Sydney was carded. I was too." I shrug. "Somehow that woman snuck in under the radar."

"That girl has tried the same trick before." He looks back at the dance floor. "I recognized her from the last time I sent her home. You'd think the staff could be on top of shit like that."

180

TROUBLEMAKER   *Deborah Bladon*

"Maybe their boss should have a word with them."

He studies me for a minute. "Maybe their boss should ask his best friend what she's doing in a club looking like sex in heels."

I blush. I feel it before I realize what's happening. "You're too charming for your own good."

"We both know that's not true." He rubs his forehead. "I'm too old for this shit. I hire people to handle this for me."

"Is that why you're here? To make sure kids don't make it past the burly bodyguard at the door?" I pick up his glass and take a small sip. The liquor burns my throat but I welcome the warmth.

"I'll get you a drink." He taps his hand on the bar and Penny, one of the bartenders instantly turns in our direction.

"No." I wave her away with a flick of my wrist. "I have to work in the morning. I can't drink."

He nods before he downs what's left in his glass in a single swallow. "I have to work in the morning too. That's why I drink."

I laugh. "It's funny how we both ended up here tonight."

He slides his hand to cover mine on the bar. "Seeing as how it's only the second time we've been here at the same time, I'd say that's fate."

I don't correct him. There's no need to. I've always been invisible to him. He's noticing me now and that's enough for me. At least I want it to be.

181

Chapter 32

Adley

"I dropped by the club to pick up some monthly statements from the office." Crew takes my keys from my hand so he can open my apartment door. "I thought I'd have one drink and then I saw that teenager trying to knock the socks off a guy that had a good ten years on her. I couldn't let it happen, legally or otherwise."

I smile. I like that he looks out for the people around him, even if he doesn't know them personally.

"Are you coming in?" I ask when he swings the door open.

"After you." He waves his arm in a wide arc.

I walk into my darkened apartment with him on my heel. I knew he'd come up after we kissed in the taxi on the way over. It wasn't an I-have-to-rip-your-clothes-off kind of kiss. It was gentle and warm, and when he bit my bottom lip, I felt heat pool between my legs.

"Do you want something to drink?" I toss my purse on the table.

"Scotch." He throws my keys, and they land next to my purse.

"No scotch." I kick off my heels. "Soda, lemonade or water?"

He shrugs out of his jacket and folds it over the back of the couch. "You must have something stronger than lemonade."

"I don't and besides, you don't need it."

182

TROUBLEMAKER   *Deborah Bladon*

His eyes sweep over my body. "We're going to fuck tonight."

My core clenches from those words. "Are we?"

He stalks toward me while he removes his cufflinks. "If you're not ready for that, I'll feast on your cunt."

I fist my hands by my side to stifle the urge to touch myself. "I love your mouth."

"You'll love it more when you're coming all over it."

I take a step back toward the couch to stabilize myself. When I finally bump into it with the back of my legs, I reach back to hold onto it.

"I could smell you on my hand the entire drive back to New York." He unbuttons each of the buttons on his shirt with effortless ease, his eyes never leaving my face. "It was driving me mad. I almost pulled over to the side of the road so I could take a taste."

I bite back a moan.

"Take off your dress."

I look at the door to my apartment. "Sydney might come home."

"Sydney won't be home for hours. She's nursing her broken heart in a private booth in the VIP room."

"With who and how do you know that?" My hands jump to my hips.

"That was the club's manager I was texting when we were in the elevator on the way up here. I told him to keep an eye on her. You seemed concerned about her when you said goodbye to her."

183

"That's nice of you," I say genuinely.

"She could use the chaperone. A woman with a wounded heart is prone to making mistakes she'll regret."

I nod as I watch him stalk closer to where I am. "Have you broken a lot of hearts?"

His fingers toy with the necklace around my neck. "A few, but they've always been fine after a brief period of mourning."

I doubt that. I wouldn't be surprised if there are dozens of women in this city wishing they could be more to him than a single night of fun.

His hands move from my neck to my shoulders. "I won't break your heart."

I stare into his eyes. I see truth there. He wants to believe that because he knows that the alternative is the end of us, as lovers, as friends, as everything.

"I won't forgive you if you do," I say quietly.

"I know," he answers in a whisper. "That's why I'll protect it at all costs."

I want to believe him. I have to if I'm going to share my body with him.

The pad of his thumb brushes my bottom lip. "I felt you in the club tonight before I saw you."

"You did?" I'm not surprised. It's been that way for me for months now. Whenever he approaches, I can feel an uptick in the restless energy in the air.

"Something changed." His hand moves lower, caressing my chin before it moves to my neck, sending shivers down my spine. "I could sense you were close. Everything quieted and then I turned around and there you were."

TROUBLEMAKER   *Deborah Bladon*

"You picked me out of a crowd of people with ease."

"Put a thousand people in front of me and I could find you with my eyes closed." He leans down to kiss me softly before his lips trail a path to my ear over my cheek. "Your smell, your voice, the pull of my body to yours; it's all real."

It is. I feel it too.

His hands make easy work of the buttons on the front of my dress. He hisses out his approval when his eyes land on my red lace bra.

"Are your panties red too?"

I nod. "It's a matching set."

He smiles before he drops to his knees. His breath feathers over my skin as he hikes the skirt of my dress up to the top of my thighs. "This is what I want."

I reach for his head to steady myself. My body arches toward him, seeking any contact. I'm so aroused, so needy.

He looks up, his eyes locking on mine. "Do you want me to taste your cunt?"

The words make me dizzy. They're so direct, and unfiltered. His eyes are filled with heavy need. "Yes."

He skims his fingers over the rough lace. "You're wet, Adley. Were you wet all night?"

I nod. "You know you make me wet."

"Was it the kiss in the taxi?"

"Yes," I purr. "It was that and when you pressed your cock into me in the hallway outside my door."

TROUBLEMAKER   *Deborah Bladon*

He did that. While I searched for my keys in my purse, he hovered behind me, his hands braced on the wall on either side of my door, his erection pulsing against my ass.

He moves his hands slowly, grabbing the waistband of my panties. He slides them lower and my breath stops. I close my eyes because this is the first time he'll see me, bare and ready for him.

"You're beautiful." He tosses the panties behind him before he blows a breath of air over my wetness. "So fucking beautiful."

The room spins when he moves. It's so quick that I can't register what's happening. Then I'm hauled over his shoulder. His hand smacks my ass and he carries me down the hallway to my bedroom, slamming the door behind us with a kick from his foot.

Chapter 33

Crew

I throw her on the bed on her back. My cock is harder than it's ever been. I want to be inside her, fucking little sounds of pleasure from her throat. Then I want in her mouth so I can blow my load on her tongue, on her lips, and on her beautiful face.

I shrug off my shirt, but I claw at her dress. She helps, twisting and turning to get herself out of it. Once she does, I toss it on the floor at my feet.

She's beautiful like this. Her tits covered in red lace, her cunt exposed and wet.

I get on the bed and kiss her lips. She moans with the touch of my mouth to hers.

I move down, grazing my teeth between her glorious tits, down her stomach until I reach the top of her cleft.

I inhale the sweet smell of her before I take my first taste.

One lick that's long and slow along the seam of her pussy lips.

Her legs fall open. "Crew, please."

It's a needy request. Her hands weave into my hair. I welcome that. I want her to guide me, to show me what she likes.

I lick her silken skin again. The taste is pure sweetness.

Her hips circle, a wanton lure for me to taste more, to savor and enjoy.

I press my hand on her stomach to hold her in place before I suck her swollen clit between my lips.

She cries out, her hands gripping the sheet beneath her. "Oh, God, oh God."

It's a chant I want to fall from her tongue for days. Fuck do I want to hear that.

I lick her, suck her, bite her and tease her with the very tip of my tongue until she's writhing beneath me, the words morphing into throaty sounds that come from deep within.

I groan into her slick flesh because my cock is so hard, my balls are drawing up just from the taste of her.

I lick a finger before I slide it into her slick channel. She tenses around me, so I drive another in, and then another.

She screams, and I know I have her. She's so close, so fucking close and when her fingers tug on my hair, and I circle back to suck on her clit, she gives me exactly what I want.

***

"Wait, wait, wait," she moans when I take off her bra and lick her right nipple. "It's too much."

"Fuck that." I laugh as I bite her.

"Oh…"

That's all I need to hear. I cradle the pebbled peak between my teeth, my tongue lashing against it.

"I just came. Let me breathe."

"I told you I was going to fuck you tonight," I say it against her breast. "We're just starting."

TROUBLEMAKER   *Deborah Bladon*

I move back and stand at the foot of her bed. I toe out of my shoes; rid myself of my socks and pants before I push my boxers down.

Her eyes are trained on my cock. She doesn't say anything. I don't need to hear words of appreciation from her. She's squirming, her thighs rubbing together in an effort to quell her need. That's all the affirmation I need that she likes what she sees.

"I don't have a condom."

That draws a smile to her lips. It should. I've never been without one, but tonight I saw no reason to tuck one into my pocket. I didn't think I'd see her and since she's the only woman I want, a condom wasn't a necessity.

She rolls on her side giving me a profile view of her plump ass. My hand circles my dick for a long, slow pull.

"I have some." She yanks open a drawer on her nightstand and fishes out a package of condoms.

I close my eyes against the visual of her doing the same with another man.

"I can put it on for you." She sits upright, ripping the package open easily.

I take it from her and slide it over my dick, without thought, just as I've done thousands of times before.

I crawl back on the bed and hover above her. I notch the head of my cock against her sex.

She's slick and ready, warm and inviting.

I push her thighs apart and sink in, not slowly but with a force so strong that it drives her small body up the twisted sheets.

TROUBLEMAKER   *Deborah Bladon*

She grabs my back, pushing herself against me, wanting the friction so she can get herself off again.

I let her use me, twisting and grinding her cunt over my cock, her head falling from side-to-side as I pump into her with steady, slow-as-hell strokes meant to drive her mad.

She whimpers and then a *fuck*, a *damn*, and *goddammit Crew*, falls from her swollen pink lips as she pants breathlessly.

I keep the same pace even though every cell in my body wants to rip her in two with drives from my cock.

"Harder," she whispers as she closes her eyes. "Christ, please, harder."

I give her exactly what she wants. I fuck her hard, recklessly, roughly until tears wet the corners of her eyes and she comes with a heady cry and a slice of her fingernails down my back.

Then I fist the flesh of her hip, hold her down and fuck my way to the most intense orgasm I've ever had as she stares into my eyes.

Chapter 34

Crew

"Crew?"

Her voice surprises me enough that I flinch when I hear it. I turn toward where she's standing in the hallway outside her bedroom.

Her hair is still a mess, her lips swollen from my kisses and her body is relaxed and hidden under an oversized pink Matiz Cosmetics T-shirt.

I left her to sleep. I couldn't stand the jackhammering that was happening in my chest. It was making me weak, so weak that I wanted to confess all my sins and secrets to her.

I can't yet. We fucked once, and although we've clearly blown the just friends line out of the water, I don't want to weigh down what's blossoming between us with shit from my past that will alter her view of who I am.

"I couldn't sleep." I pat the area on the lumpy sofa next to me.

I own this goddamn building with my brother. Our father passed it off to us in a business deal that involved us giving up stake in one of his land development companies in exchange for a portfolio of rental properties.

I lend a hand when Kade needs it, but he runs the show primarily on his own.

I hate that she lives in this dump and that her hard earned money pads my bank account.

TROUBLEMAKER   *Deborah Bladon*

She moves to where I am, sinking into the fabric. "Are you all right?"

Of course she'd ask me that after I fucked her to the edge. I left bruises on her hip, bite marks on her breast. I took because I needed to and branded her because I wanted to.

"I'm sorry if it was too much." I look at her face. She's staring at me, but her eyes have lost the wonder that was there when I entered her.

It was too fast, too much but she took it. She wanted it as desperately as I did and fuck, if I don't want to go at her again right now.

"It was perfect," she offers with a touch of her fingertips to my forearm. "Do you want to come back to bed? We can sleep for a couple more hours."

I glance down at the phone in my hand. I answered emails and made notes about today's meetings in Boston after I crawled out of her bed, put on my boxers and pants and came out here to pick up her panties and shoes.

I didn't want Sydney to see them, although she did see me when she walked in, alone, an hour ago.

There was no flirtatious look in her eye, she didn't try and flash me her lingerie. She gave me a knowing nod and went into her bedroom, closing the door behind her.

"It's almost five." I tap my finger on my phone's screen. "My day starts now."

Disappointment laces her expression. "Do you want to talk about what kept you up?"

That's a conversation that will take too long and more emotional energy than I have to give right now.

192

TROUBLEMAKER   *Deborah Bladon*

"Was I snoring?" She laughs with a hand over her mouth. "Please tell me I wasn't snoring."

"You snore?" I huff out a laugh. I'd pay good money to be witness to that. Maybe I should have stayed put and let my beating heart lull me to sleep.

"Ellie told me I did when she lived here." She fingers the hem of the T-shirt and I see her bare pussy underneath. "I'm sorry if it kept you awake."

I'd pass on sleep for the rest of my life if it meant she'd rest peacefully. I know the demons inside of her own her sleep at times, just as mine do.

"You didn't." I reach over to run my index finger over the seam of her cleft. "Let me lick this again, Ad. I want to smell like you all day."

She inches closer, allowing me to sink my finger inside.

She shudders as her hand reaches for my bare shoulder. "I'm super sore."

I nod. "Tonight, then? You can come over for dinner. I'll be back from Boston by seven and I'll eat you under the table."

"I have plans tonight."

I don't pry, even though I want to. I want to know where she is every second of the day so I can picture it in my mind and so I can rest easy knowing that what I just experienced last night won't be felt by another man ever.

"We'll talk later?" I ask with a smile. "You'll tell me all about the animals whose lives you saved today."

"Deal." She leans forward and kisses me gently. "One day maybe you can tell me why you never sleep."

TROUBLEMAKER   *Deborah Bladon*

I pull back and grab her face with both of my hands. I stare into her intense blue eyes. "I will. I promise and when I do, you'll tell me what's living inside of you and eating away at your heart."

Her eyes flicker away from mine, breaking the moment. "Last night was everything. Thank you for all of it."

"Never thank me for fucking you." I kiss her mouth, pressing my lips into hers. "You gave me more than I deserved. I'll prove to you that we can be friends and lovers."

"I want that," she whispers against my lips as her hands glide over my bare arms. "You can't know how much I want that."

I do know. It's the only fucking thing in the world that I want and I'll do whatever it takes to make certain that nothing, and no one, tears us apart.

TROUBLEMAKER   *Deborah Bladon*

Chapter 35

Adley

"How was your weekend of sun and sex?" Tilly asks as she types on the keyboard of the computer at the reception desk.

"Interesting," I answer with a sigh. I'm not about to go into details of what Crew and I did intimately. I'm also not about to talk about Damaris. That's a topic that's too ripe for gossip. If I tell Tilly about the awkward moments when Kade showed up with Crew's ex-fiancée, the entire clinic will know about it by day's end.

"Is that a good or bad interesting?" She turns her head to look at me. "You don't seem all that happy to me. Was he good in bed or not?"

I try to ignore the way she's glaring at me with expectation in her eyes. "I'm not talking about Crew's performance with you."

"I'll tell you about the last guy I was with if you want." She winks. "We can share stories of misery and missed orgasms."

"I never said anything about missing an orgasm."

She twists her chair completely to look right at me. "You two are friends first, right?"

I nod. She knows that from the times that Crew has walked through the door to say hi to me in the middle of the day.

The first time it happened, she pressed me for details about who he was, and I answered quickly that

195

he was just a friend. The skepticism in her expression was enough to tell me that she didn't believe a word I said. That changed when I set them up for their one and only disastrous date.

"I think that's the best foundation ever for a successful relationship."

Her words surprise me. I thought she'd launch into an emotional lecture about all the things that can go wrong when you sleep with a friend.

Tilly is smart with her heart. She's also yearning for a family of her own since her twin sister took the plunge last year and welcomed a baby girl three months after saying I do to her childhood sweetheart.

"I'm not sure where we're headed." I pick up the file of a pet snake that is set to slither through the door with its owner in five minutes. "We're taking it day-by-day."

"He's a catch, Ad." She turns back to the computer. "I hope that day-by-day turns into forever for you."

***

"So you and Crew?" Ellie takes a bite of a pear. "Tell me about that."

I knew this was coming. Ellie has been working part-time for the police department. She was on as a full-time employee but decided to cut back to part-time for the summer and the remainder of her pregnancy.

TROUBLEMAKER   *Deborah Bladon*

She's on shift today but called me an hour ago demanding I meet her for lunch. It wasn't rude. It was firm.

I haven't given her any details about Crew and me in the text message exchanges we've had since I got back from the Hamptons.

"We like hanging out." I take a bite of the apple she brought me. I didn't have the energy to pack a lunch today. I went back to bed after Crew left and when my alarm went off, I pushed the snooze button twice before I jumped in the shower and got ready in a hurry.

"You're going to need to do better than that, Ad." She sighs.

I shrug. "He's fun?"

She takes a deep breath, her eyes scanning my face. "It's complicated, isn't it?"

It doesn't need to be. We like each other, the sex is beyond amazing and we're clear on how important it is to talk about where things are, so our friendship doesn't go down in flames if we do.

"Every relationship has its issues, Bean."

"This one is different." She wraps the pear core in a paper napkin she brought with her to the park. "We're all a family. My kids need you both. If something goes wrong…"

I reach for her hand across the table and give it a quick squeeze. "He makes me feel safe, Ellie. He looks at me like no man has ever before and I love that. I love how I feel when I'm with him."

"Nolan loves him like a brother." She traces her finger over my palm. "I love him too. I don't want your heart to get broken if it doesn't last."

197

Ellie has always been the more cautious one. It stems from her tumultuous childhood, the death of her sister and her broken engagement to a jerk she moved to Las Vegas to marry. It wasn't until she met Nolan that she found her center. He's given her more joy these past two years than she felt in the twenty-four years before that. She deserves that level of happiness more than anyone.

"I don't know if it will last," I say honestly, biting back my emotions. "I do know that if I don't take the chance to see where this could go, that I'll regret it for the rest of my life."

"I believe you belong together. I've always felt that but now that's it's reality I'm freaking out. "She laughs softly. "I'll kill him if he breaks your heart."

She could do it, literally, with her bare hands. "He won't break my heart."

"He better not. I know where he lives."

I laugh. "Don't worry about me, Bean. Whatever happens, I've got your shoulder to cry on."

"I have two of them." She taps her hand on her left shoulder, and then the right one. "Don't ever forget how much I love you."

I can't. I won't. I love her just as much.

TROUBLEMAKER   *Deborah Bladon*

Chapter 36

Crew

"There's no fucking way that you're in my office right now." I look back at my assistant. "Nancy, you're fired."

She rolls her eyes because she's heard it before. She knows it's my go-to phrase when I'm pissed as hell. I am now because Damaris Costa is standing in my office with her hands on her hips looking like the little princess she thinks she is.

"What the ever loving fuck is going on?" I direct that question to Nancy who has now conveniently buried her nose in a magazine. "Why is she here?"

Nancy looks up at me. "She said you almost married her. That in itself is hard to believe, but then she talked about your brother. It sounded legit enough that I thought you'd want to hear what she has to say."

"What is that?" I point my finger to the wall opposite where I'm standing.

She cranes her neck to get a better look. "That's the reception couch."

"You didn't think maybe you could put it to use today and tell the Wicked Witch of the Upper East Side to park her ass there?"

"Your office door was open." She sighs. "I told her to stay put, but that's when she told me you two had been engaged once and you wouldn't mind."

"The reason I do mind is because we were engaged once." I curl my fingers around the edge of

199

her desk. "When I'm out of the office, no one is to step foot in there. Is that understood?"

Her brow furrows as she scrunches her nose. The woman has to be as old as my mother, but she tries to pass herself off as late-thirties. It's not convincing. "You're really angry this time, aren't you?"

I nod. "Keep everyone out of my office unless I am in there. Understood?"

"Understood," she repeats back meekly. "I need to run some files to Mr. Black's office. Should I do that now?"

"Nolan," I correct. "Call him Nolan and go."

She's on her feet faster than she is on Friday afternoon at five o'clock. I watch her dart to the bank of elevators I just came from, and then I turn back to look at my worst mistake.

"Hey, baby," Damaris sing-songs. "Have you missed me as much as I've missed you?"

***

"Why are you here?" I push past her to my desk. I rest both hands on it, drawing in deep breaths that can't seem to fill my lungs. "I don't want you here."

"You didn't look happy at the Hamptons house." She trails a finger down the back of my suit jacket.

I feel visibly nauseous from the touch. "Hands, Damaris. Remove your hands from me."

"Baby." Her voice grates on my last nerve. "It doesn't have to be like this. We can go back to having fun."

TROUBLEMAKER   *Deborah Bladon*

It was fun until it was a fucked up nightmare of epic proportions. "It does need to be like this and I'm not interested."

"Your little blonde friend might be."

That turns me on my heel. I stare at her. She's dressed in a crisp white blouse, matching pants, and shoes. It's in stark contrast to her dark hair and eyes. She hasn't changed at all since I pushed her out of my life four years ago. "Don't talk about her. You don't get to mention her."

"Kade said you're just friends." She coughs up a laugh. "As if I needed him to tell me that. She's clearly not your type."

She's wasting my time and my breath. I don't need this bullshit in my life. I walked away from her because I saw the evil that lives inside of her firsthand. She manipulated my pain to take anything she could from me. "You need to leave and stay gone."

"Your blonde friend would never satisfy you the way I did."

I look down at her. "Shut up, Damaris. You need to shut the hell up."

"She's more Kade's type, don't you think?" She taps her finger on her chin.

"She's too good for him."

"I think she's perfect for him." The silver bracelets on her wrist jingle as she lifts her hand. "Maybe I'll arrange a lunch and discuss that with her. There's no good reason why Adley York and I can't be friends."

The fact that she dropped Adley's full name is a warning. I know how she operates. I know what she

201

TROUBLEMAKER   *Deborah Bladon*

craves and it has nothing to do with sex and everything to do with money. "I'm not giving you another dime, Damaris."

"Did I ask for a hand-out?"

She didn't and judging by the clothes on her back and the expensive shoes on her feet, she's found someone to keep her happy.

"Stay away from Adley." I warn. "I don't want you near her."

"Any friend of yours is a friend of mine." She picks up her clutch from my desk. "I didn't come here to talk about any of that. I came to tell you that I'm working for Kade now so we'll see each other at the board meetings."

"We won't." I round my desk to put distance between us. "Only board members are allowed in those meetings, not employees."

"We shall see."

I don't give two fucks if she's in a board meeting. I usually show up at the Benton tower across town late. Then I spend the time I am forced to sit there making notes on my tablet about Matiz business. Typically, I'm out the door before the meeting is adjourned.

"Are we done?"

"I never wanted us to be."

I don't acknowledge that with a response. She was someone I was drawn to for reasons that have nothing to do with love or happiness. She was a warm and willing body when my world shattered. I held onto her to help me coast through the aftermath of that and when I finally found my way back to the

202

TROUBLEMAKER   *Deborah Bladon*

surface, I realized that we were wrong for each other in ways that had damaged us both beyond repair.

"Leave, Damaris." I point out the open door of my office. "Don't come back."

 She glances at the door before she looks back at me. "I'm glad we ran into each other in the Hamptons. It reminded me of all the good times."

I don't respond. I don't want to think about the time we spent together. Damaris is my past. Adley is my future. Neither of those points is up for discussion.

Chapter 37

Adley

"I told you I had plans." I stand in the doorway to my apartment. "I need to leave in a few minutes, Crew."

I didn't expect to see him. I told him last night after he got back from Boston that I had plans for tonight too and yet here is, with a bouquet of wildflowers in hand and a devilish grin on his face.

"I brought these so Sydney could put them by your bedside." He brushes past me. "I suppose now that you're here, I can do it myself."

"I'll do it." I reach for the vase and tug it from him. "Thank you for these, but it wasn't necessary."

"It was necessary." He leans forward to give me a soft kiss on the lips. "I want you to wake up to something beautiful every morning."

It's a sweet sentiment, and at any other time, I'd tell him that I would love to wake up to the sight of his handsome face, but right now my focus is singular and it's not on him. "I wish you would have called first."

Those words send his brows shooting up. "Why is that?"

I move to set the vase down on my coffee table. I'm agitated. It started this afternoon with a woman who made it clear to the entire clinic that she thinks I suck majorly at my job. Then I missed the train I wanted to catch to come home, so I had to board a bus, which was overcrowded. I made it home

TROUBLEMAKER *Deborah Bladon*

with just a few minutes to spare, so I changed into a simple outfit of black pants and a white blouse without the benefit of a shower or any makeup beyond a light coat of mascara and a swipe of clear gloss over my lips.

"You knew I had plans."

"I didn't think you would be here."

He's right. It's not as though he made a point of coming over here to distract me on purpose. "I'm sorry, Crew. I'm on edge."

He moves to rest his hands on my shoulders. It does little to calm me. It just notches up my uneasiness in an entirely different way. I'm still sore from what we did two nights ago. The ache between my legs is nothing compared to the pounding of my heart when I feel his hands on me.

How could I not want a man who made me feel things I've never felt before?

"Take a deep breath." He bends at the knees to rest his forehead against mine. "Slow and steady breaths, Ad."

My phone chimes on the table next to the vase.

I rush away from him to pick it up. I read the message and it just ups the tempo of my heart all over again. "That's the driver. I need to go."

"A driver?" He walks over to where I'm standing, canting his head to get a look at my phone. "You ordered a car?"

"No." I shake my head. "John sent it."

"Ad." He touches my chin and tilts my head up so our eyes meet. "Assure me again that John is not someone I need to punch in the throat."

TROUBLEMAKER   *Deborah Bladon*

I laugh because his smile says more than his words. "He's helping me figure out a few things."

"That's cryptic." He stands back and looks at me. "I'm always here to talk too. You know I'm the best problem solver around."

I drop my gaze. "It's not a problem. It's a dream."

"A dream?" He moves closer pulling me into his strong embrace. "What dream?"

A soft knock on my apartment door takes me from his arms. I cross the room quickly and swing open the door to see the familiar face of John Tate's driver.

"I need to go." I look back at Crew. "I can do anything I set my mind to, right?"

"You know it." He moves toward me with a confident stride. "I believe in you more than I believe in anyone. Follow your dreams, Adley. I'm right beside you every step of the way."

"You don't know what the dream is yet," I whisper as I arch up on my heels to kiss him.

"It doesn't matter what it is. You'll make it come true."

***

I take a shortcut through the Emergency Room after spending more than three hours on the seventh floor of the hospital. I shared the elevator ride down with two doctors and a nurse who talked in low whispers about a patient that will be moved to hospice care tomorrow.

TROUBLEMAKER   *Deborah Bladon*

We might not have the same jobs, but I know all about death. I've had to watch people crumble when they've heard the news that their cat didn't make it. I've listened to the wails of children after being told that their dog would never come back home.

Death is a part of medicine. It's a sad but integral part of the cycle of life, and I'm strong enough to handle it. I know I am.

The elevator dings our arrival on the first floor and when the doors swing open the mad rush of the ER is what greets us.

Both doctors head straight for the reception desk. I have no idea if they are ER physicians or not. What I do know is that every single person who works in this building plays a pivotal role in patient care. It doesn't matter if it's the head of cardiology or the people who work tirelessly in the kitchen. They all are essential to the well-being of those who come here for help.

I scan the area. The noise and frenetic energy don't overwhelm me. I take comfort in the knowledge that there are trained professionals who will do their best to help everyone here.

I take a step forward while I dig in my purse for my phone to order an Uber to pick me up.

John offered to call his driver to take me home, but I insisted on finding my own way. When he rushed off for an emergency consultation in the ER, I stayed back and spoke to a surgeon for ten minutes until he too, had to run to help someone who needed him.

"Adley?" A familiar male voice pulls my gaze to the left.

207

TROUBLEMAKER   *Deborah Bladon*

I search the faces of the people standing near the reception desk. Every one of them is looking for an answer to an urgent question.

"Over here." The voice calls again and I shift my focus more to the right and when I do my eyes land right on him.

"Kade?" I say his name as I move toward him, brushing past a woman with dark hair who is rushing in with a child in her arms.

"What are you doing…" I start to ask what he's doing in the ER at eleven o'clock at night, but my words get caught in my throat when I look past where he's standing to see the face of Crew's sister, his mother and his older brother, Curtis. I've met Lark before but I recognize the others from the photographs in Crew's apartment.

"Kade." I reach for him once I'm close enough. "Where's Crew?"

He points to a corridor that I know leads to a series of exam rooms. "There. He's down there."

I steady Kade's shaking hand in my own. I draw a deep breath because whatever it is, Crew is strong. "What's happened?"

"You don't know?" He scans my face looking for an answer to a question I'm not aware of. I don't know why any of the Benton family is here.

I crane my neck to look down the corridor but it's just a steady stream of medical personnel going in and out of cubicles. "No. What happened to Crew?"

I bite the corner of my lip suddenly overcome with a rush of emotions. He can't be hurt. I can't breathe if he's hurt. I need him. I care about him so much.

208

TROUBLEMAKER   *Deborah Bladon*

I think I love him.

"It's our dad." His voice breaks as he buries his face in his hands. "He had a heart attack. It doesn't look good."

TROUBLEMAKER 　　　　　　*Deborah Bladon*

Chapter 38

Crew

I stand in the exam room with my hands in the pockets of my pants staring at the frail man on the stretcher. He's hooked up to machines that monitor his heart, oxygen is being pumped into his nose, and his gray eyes look sunken and cloudy.

"You came," he whispers when he finally notices me standing at the foot of the stretcher.

I came as soon as my sister, Lark, called me. I was having dinner by myself at an Italian place a block from my apartment. I was staring at my phone. The temptation to call Bill was pressing.

I've held off asking him where he took Adley the other day when he picked her up outside her apartment. I wanted to know tonight, but just as I was about to make the call, Lark called me in a panic.

I paid the check, walked out of the restaurant and hailed the first taxi I saw to bring me here.

"You knew I would," I answer quietly. "I'm always there if someone from the family needs me."

It's the truth. Even when my asshole of a younger brother is in need, I'm there for him. I have been there for all of them since day one. I will always be there for them.

"I might not make it this time."

He's right. The doctor who first examined him told us as much. His heart is failing. He's already lived through a minor heart attack. This one is a tsunami compared to that one.

210

TROUBLEMAKER *Deborah Bladon*

He was in his office, heading a meeting when he collapsed face first on the boardroom table. It's a fitting slice of irony.

The man who will push anyone aside to make a dollar, falls victim to his greed and the stress that comes with it.

"You have a great doctor, dad."

I test the water, but the shark, even in his weakened state, strikes.

"Sir."

I bark out a laugh. It stopped hurting years ago, long after the first subtle correction at the dinner table when I was an innocent kid, excitedly telling his parents about a science award.

"Call me sir, Crew. That's what I want all my boys to do."

He has three boys, yet only two are allowed to call him dad; the two who were born with his blood running through their veins.

He's dad to Lark as well, but never to me. Not in any significant way.

I say what I've always wanted to say to him because for him there may not be a sunrise tomorrow. "I forgive you."

"For what?" Both his graying brows rise. "Forgive me for what? I gave you a better life than anyone else could have."

In his eyes he has.

I was adopted because my birth mother, a single French woman, couldn't handle me.

I was a troublemaker she'd tell my father every day when she showed up to work for him as his

211

secretary twenty-six years ago. Until one day when she didn't show up at all.

She gave me up that day. I was three-years-old.

Foster care was my home until my mother, Pauline Benton, convinced her husband, Eli, to take me in. They ran through the process to become my foster parents, and eventually my adoptive parents when my birth mother's rights were willfully terminated because she left me without so much as a glance back.

Her family back in Paris wanted nothing to do with her, or me.

I began this life as Jordan Fournier.

I live my life as Crew Benton.

"For everything," I answer his question.

"If I ever raised a hand to you..." He stops to hold his hand against his chest, his face twisting in pain. "I did my best with you. You were never like your brothers. You were always getting in trouble."

I was a typical child who tested the limits and explored without any thought to consequence. The biggest crime in his eyes is that I'm a Benton by default, not by design.

"I'm going to grant your dying wish." I walk to the side of the bed and stand over him.

He stares up at my face. There's not an ounce of tenderness in his eyes. That's reserved for his grandchildren and his children. It's never been directed at me.

"The company? You'll sign your shares over to me?"

TROUBLEMAKER   *Deborah Bladon*

I laugh because he's about to endure a surgery he may not survive. "To Lark."

His brow furrows and his hand presses harder against his chest. "She works at Matiz. She knows nothing about what we do at Benton. She already has enough shares. If you give her yours and I die, she'll have controlling interest."

"As it should be. She's more equipped to run that ship than anyone else." I lean down and kiss his forehead. "You've been a bastard to me, old man. You should have given me a chance because I loved you. All I wanted was to be loved back."

Before he can respond, I stalk across the room to the curtain that separates the exam room from the corridor and I leave behind the man who took more from me than he ever gave.

Chapter 39

Crew

I walk out of the exam room and into my mom's arms. She's a small woman, but her arms have always been the safest place on earth to me.

She's loved me without reservation from the first day we met. She read to me, taught me how to tie my shoes and when I graduated college she was in the front row screaming my name with tears streaming down her face.

I am her son as much as Kade and Curtis, my older brother, are.

"You talked to him?" She takes a step back to look up at me. "How did it go?"

"Fine, mom." I kiss the top of her head. "I said my peace. He said his. We're good now."

She's at peace too. Her life hasn't been easy. I've tried my best to offer her refuge from the storm of his temper. He's never touched her in anger. My siblings have always been safe from that too.

I wasn't as fortunate.

It was never overt. I didn't have bruises but the pushing and shoving and name calling created scars that no one can see.

"He'll need to have surgery. Kade will stay here with me." She squeezes my arms. "I want you to go home, sweetie. Take Lark with you. Her son needs her, and there's a woman who needs you."

"What woman?"

TROUBLEMAKER   *Deborah Bladon*

Her hand brushes my arm as she points into the waiting room. "That beautiful woman over there talking to your father's doctor needs you more than I do."

I look back over my shoulder and see the woman I love.

Adley is deep in conversation with Dr. John Tate, the cardiologist brought in to take over my dad's case. My mom requested him personally because of his reputation for being a leader in his field.

No one expected him to be in the hospital this late since he's not on call tonight, but he was in the cardiology ward. When I mentioned to the admitting doctor that I know Dr. Tate's daughter, Sydney, personally, he relayed the message, and within five minutes I was shaking John's hand and thanking him for his help.

I watch Adley as she plays with the hospital visitor badge strung around her neck on a lanyard. I see how focused she is on everything he's telling her.

I see her dream now.

The stack of medical books on the coffee table in her apartment.

The catalog for the New York School of Medicine that was on her kitchen counter.

The poster of the human heart hanging behind her bathroom door.

I assumed it was Sydney's dream to follow in her father's footsteps, but this is Adley's dream.

She turns toward me then, her face searching for mine. I know she feels the same connection I do and when she finally locks eyes with me, I have no

215

TROUBLEMAKER   *Deborah Bladon*

doubt that I'm looking at the future Dr. Adley York, Cardiologist.

***

"We can stay," she says softly after kissing me. "I'm fine with staying."

"He's stabilized." I look over at where Dr. Tate is speaking to my mother. "They're going to monitor him tonight and decisions will be made tomorrow. He's weak, Ad."

"He needs a double bypass." She looks into my eyes. "It's risky because of his prior myocardial infarction."

"You want this, don't you?"

The sudden subject change takes her surprise. She's silent for a moment as she digests what I just said. "You mean do I want to be a doctor?"

I nod. "I see the dream."

The corner of her mouth curves into a smile. "You do?"

"This is why you kept putting off going back to school to be a vet, isn't it?"

She rubs the edge of the badge around her neck. "Yes. I always felt a pull toward taking care of animals, but then John came over to help Sydney move in. We talked for hours about his work. I was so excited by that."

"I think it's the perfect fit for you." I reach for her hands. "You know I'm on board to help in any way I can."

Her gaze drops to the tiled floor. "It's going to eat up my entire life for the next decade. Well, forever if I'm honest. But I feel a passion for this I

TROUBLEMAKER *Deborah Bladon*

never felt when I thought about being a vet. I know this is right for me, I just have to see if I can make it my reality."

"You can do anything, Ad," I say the words with all the assurance I feel. "You're the most determined person I've ever met. You're going to ace this and one day, you'll be the doctor people will call when they want the best of the best."

She squeezes my hands tightly. "Say that again when I start doubting myself."

"Crew?" My sister walks up beside us. "I'm going to take off. I want to go home to see Ryker and Benton."

Benton Moore. My nephew. A little boy named after our family. That was a gift from Lark. She's been a gift to me. I couldn't ask for a better sister.

"You know, Adley, right?" I wrap my arm around Adley's waist.

"We met at Matiz when she came to see you one day." She smiles at Ad. "She kept me in one piece earlier. She may be the calmest person in this waiting room."

Adley laughs. "It's all smoke and mirrors."

No, it's inner strength and a strong spirit.

I want to tell her about my adoption and the hell I've been through, but tonight is for her. I won't tarnish her dream with my nightmare. At least, not tonight.

"We're heading out too." I look back at where my mom is now sitting with my brothers in a row of chairs near a vending machine. "I'll go give mom a goodnight kiss and then I'll take my two favorite women home."

Chapter 40

Adley

I feel the cool air rise from the floor when he opens the shower door. I left him in my bedroom after we got back from the hospital.

He called Bill, who came to get us and after we dropped off Lark, we sat in the back of the car holding hands in silence. I know it has to be hard for him. His father is hanging by a thread. Before we left the hospital, I asked him twice if he wanted to stay, but he was insistent that he needed to be with me. I didn't argue.

"I need you so much," he whispers those words against the shell of my ear. "I want to be close to you, inside of you. I want to feel you all around me."

I turn quickly to face him. He's already wet. The water is running over his handsome face, down his chiseled body, and trailing along his heavy, thick cock.

I want to give him pleasure more than I've wanted to before. I can see the pain in his eyes. I can feel it in his touch. He's holding himself together even though inside, I know that pieces of him are broken beyond repair.

I lower myself to my knees, slowly. "I've wanted to do this for a long time."

He groans his approval as his legs inch apart.

TROUBLEMAKER   *Deborah Bladon*

I wrap my hand around the base, the pad of my thumb rubbing the underside. I inhale his scent. Masculine, musky, mine.

I lick the crown softly, twirling my tongue around it, savoring my first taste of this glorious man.

"I'll come from this." His voice is husky as he runs his fingers through my hair. "If I fuck your mouth, I'll come."

I respond with another lash of my tongue before I slide my mouth over him.

"Yes," he hisses as his hips circle. "Just like that."

I moan around him, lost in the feeling that I'm giving him exactly what he gave to me. I suck him harder, taking him deeper down my throat as I drop one hand to rub my clit.

"Jesus, Ad." He growls. "Touch it for me."

I pull him out of my mouth and lick his shaft with soft fluttering lashes of my tongue while I work to get myself off.

"I want in on that." He hauls me up by my arms and slams my back against the shower wall.

He kisses me, hard. Hard enough to bruise my mouth as his hand brushes mine away from my core so he can take over.

He slides two fingers into me, as his thumb works on my clit.

I reach down to touch him, to stroke him and as the water beats down on us, we take each other to the edge before he turns me around, pushes my body against the wall and licks my pussy, pulling his teeth over my clit until I scream when I find my release.

220

TROUBLEMAKER   *Deborah Bladon*

***

"Crew," I pant as I say his name. "Oh, God."

He looks at me. His eyes are darkened with the desperate need to come. "More, Ad. Give me one more."

I can't. I've already come twice. Once in the shower and again, here against the wall in my bedroom.

My legs are wrapped around him. His hands are cupping my ass, and with each slam of his cock into me, the wall shakes behind us.

"Slow," I manage to get the word out. "Slower."

He kisses me softly, his tongue tracing a delicious path over my lower lip. "Slow."

I moan from the change in tempo. Until now it was desperate hard fucks, our bodies slapping together in a concert of desire, a rush to feel as much as we could.

Now, it's gentle, easy and his cock is stretching me in the most painfully delicious ways.

"You want it like this?" He licks my neck. "Just like this?"

I nod because my voice is lost in the need to come again. I'm close, so fucking close.

"You are everything," he whispers into the flesh of my neck.

He is. He's everything.

Hope, promise, love and every tomorrow.

"Look at me, Ad." He moves so his face is almost touching mine. "Let me see your face when you come."

TROUBLEMAKER   *Deborah Bladon*

I don't try and hide it. I stare into his beautiful green eyes.

I grind against him, taking in the way he wants me to; uninhibited, unafraid, and unashamed.

"Crew," I say his name as my core clenches when the ripples of my orgasm wash over me. He's captivated, his eyes never leaving my face.

My hands grip his strong shoulders tightly as I fall from the high.

"Fuck, that was beautiful." He trails kisses over my neck. "My turn."

He lowers me to my feet, turns me around and fucks me hard to his own release.

TROUBLEMAKER *Deborah Bladon*

Chapter 41

Adley

"I need to go to work." I push on his shoulder. "Crew? Wake up. I need to go."

He lazily opens his eyes before kicking back the blanket. "Since when do you go to work before five a.m?"

"It's almost nine." I stare at his nude body. I fell asleep in his arms after we made love. I listened to his steady breathing for more than an hour before I finally drifted off too.

"What?" He sits upright, raking both hands through his hair. "What the hell? I never sleep past five a.m."

"Never say never, Benton," I quip. "There's coffee in the kitchen. Sydney will probably offer you half of her breakfast, and she'll be wearing nothing but lingerie. I suggest you don't take up either of those offers."

He wiggles his brows. "I'm only hungry for one thing."

"I can't be late." I tap my shoe on the floor. "I called Kade an hour ago. He said your dad is stable. They'll run some tests this morning, and then Dr. Tate will advise them about whether surgery is a viable option at this time."

"Thanks for the update, Dr. York."

I smile broadly. "I'm going to do it. I want it."

"You'll do it." He pulls his arms over his head in a stretch. Sweet Jesus, those biceps make me want

223

TROUBLEMAKER   *Deborah Bladon*

to crawl back in bed. "Why were you so secretive about it? You could have just told me that you're going to be a doctor."

I risk being five minutes late and sit on the edge of the bed. "I needed to believe I could do it before I told anyone."

He leans back against the wooden headboard. I know he's waiting for me to explain more.

"When I first entertained the idea, it felt like it was too much to hope for." I smooth my palms over the thighs of my scrubs. "I could see this mountain in front of me and it seemed insurmountable. I knew if I told you or Ellie, you'd tell me to chase the dream, but what good would that be if I didn't believe in myself?"

"You believe in yourself now." He searches my gaze. "I saw it at the hospital last night. You were standing there talking to John like you belonged there. You looked at home there."

"I felt that." I reach for his forearm. "John has been taking me on small tours of the cardiology department. He had a mentor who did the same for him before he went to medical school. It convinced him that he was doing the right thing by investing so much of his life in his passion. I feel that too."

"Whatever you need from me to make this a reality, you have it."

I know that. I knew it before he offered. I've looked into student loans and I've been saving like mad so I can get myself through school. "I have most everything covered but I'm going to need your emotional support. I need you in my corner telling me that all the long hours and sacrifices are worth it."

224

TROUBLEMAKER   *Deborah Bladon*

"You can count on me." He leans forward to kiss me softly. "I'm here today and when you graduate as Dr. York, I'll be there beside you."

I want that. I want him to take this journey with me, not as a friend, but as more.

"I need to get to work." I kiss him again, deeper this time, my tongue tracing a path over his lips. "Will I see you tonight?"

"You better believe it." He reaches to cup my face. "I'm so fucking crazy about you, Adley. You know that, don't you? You feel it."

I feel love. It's nothing like what I felt for Leo. This is different. It's consuming and comforting. It's where I belong.

"I feel all of it."

"I'll come back here at seven. Does that work for you?"

"I'll meet you at the hospital at seven," I counter.

Last night it felt like he was struggling over what's going on with his dad. We left the hospital quickly and he's made no effort to check in with Kade or anyone in his family since.

"Seven at the hospital it is."

"I'll meet you at the nurses' desk on the seventh floor."

"Seventh floor at seven." He taps his forehead. "Got it."

I move to stand but his hand grabs my wrist.

"Kiss me one last time, Ad."

I do. I kiss him slowly and when I pull back, I see forever in his eyes.

225

TROUBLEMAKER   *Deborah Bladon*

***

"You're Hale's babe, aren't you?"

I look over at the man standing next to the exam table holding the leash of a Boston Terrier. He can't be much older than I am. "I'm not."

"Yes, you are," he insists with a grin. "I follow those posts religiously and I know she works here. You're her."

This isn't the first or even the second, time this has happened since I stopped seeing Trey. Unfortunately, he hasn't started dating again, so those posts are still the first that pop up whenever anyone searches for the halesbabe hashtag.

I'm not going to stand here and argue the point. It's useless. "I was seeing Trey, but it's over now."

"So you're available?" He shoves a hand through his short blond hair.

"No," I answer quickly. "I'm not."

"You're sure?" He leans forward and his hot breath skirts over my cheek. I step back, wishing I would have broken clinic policy and left the door to the exam room open.

"I'm positive." I cast my gaze down to the tablet in my shaking hands. "I'm going to go see what's keeping Dr. Hunt."

He steps in front of me as I walk toward the door. "Don't rush off, Adley."

I hate that I was tagged in any of those photographs. I never wanted my face out there. I like to live my life in private, quietly. "Please move aside."

TROUBLEMAKER   *Deborah Bladon*

He doesn't move. "I'm still a member. I remember the first time I ever saw you there."

Panic creeps down my spine. This can't be happening again. Please, not again.

"I don't know what you're talking about." My voice is as unsteady as my hands. "If you'll move aside, I can get the doctor."

"I'm talking about Club Skyn, Social Room A. You laid out like a feast for anyone who wanted…"

The door flies open and Dr. Hunt marches in with a smile on his face and his usual greeting. "Good morning, who do we have here?"

He stops as soon as his eyes lock on mine."Adley? What's wrong?"

I shake my head as I try and speak. "I need to take a minute."

Dr. Hunt brushes next to the man to reach for my hand. "Go to the lunchroom. Sit. I'll be in to check on you as soon as I'm done here."

I nod and as I start to walk away, I hear the bastard's voice trailing behind me. "It was good to see you again, Adley. You know where to find me."

227

TROUBLEMAKER   *Deborah Bladon*

Chapter 42

Crew

Some people will tell you that money can't buy happiness. They may be right, but today it bought me peace of mind, two-fold.

My lawyer worked out a deal with Lucia. I wouldn't accept the lowball offers she was volleying my way, so I countered with an offer of my own to take over her shares of the club.

She sent me a few video text messages I ignored, then she called and left a voicemail message telling me how much she missed riding me reverse cowgirl while staring out at the strip through the windows of my hotel suite. I deleted that and her number from my phone.

Finally, she relented and took my deal.

It was a steep price to pay for a missed fuck, but the lesson was invaluable and learned too late. Never mix business with pleasure.

I followed the rule religiously until I met Lucia.

Since Ad is going to be a doctor and I can't stand the sight of blood, I'll never have to worry about the business/pleasure mix again.

"Ms. Costa is here to see you," Nancy announces from the doorway of my office like any good assistant would. The eye roll she gifts me with is the cherry on the sundae.

"Sit, Damaris."

TROUBLEMAKER   *Deborah Bladon*

I don't rise from my chair because respect isn't part of the dynamic of my relationship with this woman.

"You're tense, Crew. You need a good fuck."

Nancy tiptoes backward out of the doorway when she hears those words coming out of the mouth of my ex-fiancée.

"Leave the door open," I call after her. "The witch has to catch a broom out of town at three. She won't be staying long."

I hear Nancy's muffled laugh as Damaris takes a seat in front of my desk.

"You heard about my promotion?" She edges her finger over the corner of her lip.

I arranged the fucking thing and I would call it more a banishing than a promotion. It was my last official duty as a shareholder at Benton Holdings. Lark is taking over my shares tomorrow, even though Eli is still clinging to the last edges of his life with desperation.

"You're going to Italy." I tap my hand on the top of my desk. "Look whose dream is coming true."

She tilts her chin up. "I've always wanted to live in Rome. Now, I get to run the entire division of Benton's sales offices there."

It's one office that employs one person. That individual will be relocated back to Belgium. It's a move they've been desperately wanting for months.

"Will you miss me?" She smiles tightly.

"I didn't miss you before I saw you in the Hamptons, Damaris. Why the fuck would I miss you now?"

229

"There was a time when I thought we would make it."

If I ever felt that it was fleeting. The highs of the sex and the lows of the pain I was in made it impossible to see a day ahead of me. I clung to Damaris because she was a warm body who kept me afloat.

"We weren't good for one another." I take a deep breath. "We would have destroyed each other."

"It would have been a hell of a way to go." She laughs. "I think back on what we did. It's hard to believe that was me."

Or me.

Drugs, unprotected sex, blackouts. It was all part of our daily fare.

I took chances with my safety and hers because I couldn't see through the anguish I was in. She trusted me to take care of her and when I couldn't anymore, the dynamic shifted. I needed her to take the wheel, but she couldn't handle it. She didn't have the strength.

"I want to the hospital to see your dad," she begins before she corrects herself. "Eli. I went to see Eli."

She knows. Damaris was by my side when I set out on the search to find my birth mother. She was there when I did. "I don't give a shit how that went."

She clasps her hands together on her lap. "I know, Crew. He told me he hopes all of his kids miss him when he's gone."

Of course he does. He wants the reassurance that we'll be in pain because of his death. I lie to myself that I won't, but grief is born in honesty. There

TROUBLEMAKER   *Deborah Bladon*

will be a void. It won't be because he's not there anymore, but the chance; the might have been, will be gone.

"He remembered you?" I ask to avoid addressing what she just said. "It's been almost five years."

Her face softens. "He told me that he thought I was wrong for you. Not that I was too good, mind you, but wrong. He said you need a woman who can tame you. I told him she doesn't exist."

She does and I'm in love with her.

"He's lived the life he wanted to live." I deflect. "We've made our peace."

She moves to stand, I don't follow. "Do you ever miss us, Crew?"

"No," I respond without any hesitation. I won't ask her the same question because I can see the answer in her eyes.

"I'll keep in touch with Kade. He'll know how I'm doing if you're ever interested."

He won't stay in touch.

Getting her out of New York is a move meant to keep her out of my life, and Kade's. I stopped by his office at the Benton tower yesterday. There wasn't a complaint when I told him I was sending Damaris abroad. His only request was that he wanted to be the one to tell her.

I ran through his expense reports before I signed my shares over to Lark. He's been paying the lease on Damaris's apartment in Tribeca for years, supplying her with credit cards, sending her on trips.

TROUBLEMAKER   *Deborah Bladon*

Either she's holding something over his head, or she's been in his bed. Either way, he's not torn up about her move.

She's a special kind of evil. One with a pretty face and a cold, empty heart. Once she steps on that plane this afternoon, I'll rest easy knowing that she's a continent away with her sights set on someone else.

TROUBLEMAKER   *Deborah Bladon*

Chapter 43

Adley

I see her as soon as she walks through the door of Premier Pet Care. She looks out of place in her tailored white suit, her red-bottomed heels and the small hat perched on the top of her head. Damaris looks like royalty. I look like I rolled in a pool of blood.

Another day, another blood sample from a dog who is scared of needles.

"Adley." She waves to me like we're old friends. "It's good to see you."

I can't say the same. I'm still trying to calm down after my encounter with the man who recognized me from Club Skyn.

When Donovan came to check on me in the lunchroom, he assumed it was low blood sugar that caused all the color to drain from my face and my limbs to shake.

I didn't correct him because I can't. I can't tell anyone here about what happened to me in that club or that I was even there.

"Damaris." I approach her knowing that Tilly's eyes are glued to the side of my head. "What a surprise."

I don't attach a smile to the words because I'm not happy to see her. I can only imagine that she's here to rub some sordid detail about her relationship with Crew in my face. She picked the worst possible day to drop by.

233

TROUBLEMAKER *Deborah Bladon*

"Can we talk in private?" She bends at the knees to look me square in the face like I'm a child.

"I'm very busy." I point at the waiting room. "We're booked up solid today, so maybe another time?"

I can pencil her in at noon on the day hell freezes over.

"I have something that belongs to you." She pats her oversized purse. "If we step outside I can give it to you. You can spare two minutes for a friend of Crew's, can't you?"

"You're due for a break, Ad," Tilly calls from where she's standing. "I'll cover for you."

I shoot her a look because wasting my break with Damaris is a crime. I covet those fifteen minutes twice a day and the hour at lunch. I use them to study my cardiology books. Now I have to waste a quarter of an hour on someone who I know is here to cause me heartache.

I brush past Damaris and push open the glass door of the clinic. I point to a spot on the sidewalk close to the building next door that is tucked away from the pedestrian traffic that is clipping past us at a steady pace.

She follows me in silence, her heels clicking a steady beat over the concrete.

"What is it, Damaris?" The question leaves my lips as soon I turn toward her.

"You're sleeping with him, aren't you?" She manages a small smile. "You're not just friends. It's already more."

I'm not surprised by her words. Anyone who walked in on Crew and me the other day would have

234

TROUBLEMAKER   *Deborah Bladon*

jumped to the same conclusion. Even Kade, who seemed oblivious to what we were doing, knows now after seeing the two of us together at the hospital. I kissed Crew in front of his family, and he embraced me. I have nothing to hide when it comes to how I feel about him.

"How is that your business?" I wipe my palm over a large red spot on my thigh. "Did you come here to interrogate me about Crew? If you did, you're wasting my time and yours."

She ponders that for a minute with pursed lips before her hand with its perfectly manicured red fingernails dives into her bag. "You left something in the master suite at the house in Westhampton."

I scrunch my nose as I watch her hand squirm under the expensive leather. "What is it?"

She yanks out the weathered paperback novel that my mom loaned to me for the drive up. "This. I knew it didn't belong to Pauline, so I assumed it was yours."

I snatch it from her hand and cradle it to my chest. My mom never expected me to return it. She breezes through at least four books a month and then loans them to me. It's her way of clearing out the small bookshelf in her dining room so she can add more of her temporary favorites to it.

"Thank you," I say because it's expected and I'm not an ungrateful person. "You could have just given it to Kade."

"I found it in my luggage this morning. I had to repack. I'm moving to Rome."

Okay. Sure and I don't care.

"I stopped by Crew's office to say goodbye."

235

I narrow my eyes, a sense of regret already on me for asking the question poised on the edge of my tongue. "How did that go?"

Her eyes brighten. "It was good. We talked about our past, not all of it, of course. He doesn't like to talk about certain things."

I won't push for more because she's baiting me with a hook that she thinks is irresistible to me. It's not. I've been holding tightly to a painful secret from my past. I can't expect that Crew doesn't have his own burdens to carry.

"I need to get back in there. I hope things go your way in Rome."

"Wait." Her hand reaches for mine. "I'm sorry about that night, Adley."

I brush her touch away. "It was miscommunication. Kade didn't realize that we'd still be in the Hamptons."

"No." She steps closer, her voice lowering. "Not that night."

I study her expression. It's shifted. The smug satisfaction that was in her eyes is gone. It's been replaced with sadness or maybe it's regret. I don't know her well enough to venture a guess.

"You looked so familiar to me." Her gaze skims over my face. "I thought about you since I saw you at the Hamptons and now I remember."

"Remembered what?" I lift my hand to stop her words, even though I want to hear them.

She sucks in a deep breath. "The night at the club when Crew saved you."

TROUBLEMAKER   *Deborah Bladon*

I stumble back from her words. The book falls from my hands as I claw at the brick wall next to me trying to find something to hold onto.

She takes a step toward me, closing in on me, taking away all the air that I need to breathe. "Does he not know? Why on earth wouldn't you tell him who you are?"

Because he'll see who I was then, and not who I am now and the pity will overshadow the love.

"Ad?" Tilly calls from the open door of the clinic behind me. "Your break is over. It's all hands on deck in exam room one."

I don't look at Damaris again. I pick up the book, straighten my scrubs and walk back to my life; the life I've worked so hard to build for myself.

TROUBLEMAKER　　　　　　　　　*Deborah Bladon*

Chapter 44

Adley

I'm sitting in the darkness in Crew's apartment. It's nearing nine o'clock. I didn't go to the hospital at seven. There wasn't any need to. My intention, when I told him to meet me there was simple. I wanted to ease the burden that he's been carrying for years. I don't know exactly what happened between him and his dad, but I know that their relationship is nothing like the one I have with my own father.

I wanted to meet Eli, and sing Crew's praises and maybe, just maybe, repair part of what's been broken.

I didn't get my chance.

Eli Benton took his last breath at one minute after five with his wife by his side.

Crew texted me to tell me. It was direct and to the point.

Eli is dead.

I was just leaving work, on legs that were still wobbly after my encounter with Damaris.

Her words shook me to my core.

I went back into the clinic after Tilly called me in and threw my mind and body into my job. I helped hold down a Saint Bernard that was in the clinic because of a splinter in its paw. It cried out when Dr. Hunt yanked the thing piece of wood out. I cried too and everyone assumed it was my caring nature on display yet again.

TROUBLEMAKER   *Deborah Bladon*

They were wrong. I was crying for the twenty-one-year-old girl who walked into a sex club because her boyfriend wanted it more than anything.

I hear Crew's key in the lock, but I don't turn from where I'm sitting on his sofa, my feet resting on the edge of the coffee table.

I came here straight from work because I wanted to be close to him. I knew he'd go to the hospital and spend time with his family. I didn't want to intrude. Grief is a private process for some. I know it is for Crew.

I took a shower, threw my scrubs into his washing machine and dressed in my panties and one of his T-shirts. It's too big and bulky, but it smells like him.

His keys hit the table before he rounds the corner and slows. I hear the hesitation in his steps.

"I'm sorry," I whisper. "I'm so sorry, Crew."

He stalks toward me, heavy, measured steps that don't stop until he's almost on top of me.

His arms reach out and I grab for them, letting him pull me to my feet. He doesn't speak, but his body's movements say everything. He pulls me closer, tugging my legs up until I circle them around his waist.

His lips find mine in a messy, frenzied kiss. I taste the salt of his tears as he pushes my mouth open with his tongue.

We set out on a path across the living room, down the hallway and finally to his bedroom. He lowers me onto the bed, before ridding himself of his clothes.

239

TROUBLEMAKER   *Deborah Bladon*

I stare up at him, our eyes saying more to each other than our words ever could. I know he's grieving. I know he doesn't want to. I know pain like this is what is buried beneath his calm, controlled exterior, and his sense of humor and his deep compassion.

"I need you," he rasps. "Fuck, do I need you."

I pull the shirt over my head and reach out with my hand. "I'm here, Crew."

He falls into my arms, his face awash with tears, his shoulders surging forward as he rips my panties from my body and pushes my thighs apart.

"I need to feel loved," he growls before he lashes at the seam of my pussy with his tongue. "I want to feel needed."

I stop him with two fists to his hair. I turn his head, so he's looking up at me, his warm breath trailing over my wetness. "I love you, Crew. I need you."

Tears stream down his handsome face as he licks me once more before he whispers back, "I love you, too."

***

I stretch onto my back. Every muscle in my body is tender. He went at me like an animal for hours. Bursts of gentle pleasure mixed with the pain of his hands fisting the flesh of my hips and his cock driving into me with more force than I've ever felt before.

I held him while he cried, whispered that I loved him when he pulled me into his arms, and I

TROUBLEMAKER   *Deborah Bladon*

watched him stare out into the darkness of the city when he got up to get another condom.

He finally fell asleep an hour ago.

I move to get up. I need a glass of water and more air to breathe than is left in this room.

"Ad?" he murmurs as his hand lands on my bare back. "Please don't go."

I slide closer to him. I stare at his face and his half-open eyes. "I'm not going anywhere. I'll stay all night."

"Stay forever," he whispers.

I smile. "I might have to. I don't know if my legs work anymore."

He huffs out a small laugh and it's music to my ears. "I'll carry you everywhere you need to go."

I rest my forehead against his and cup my hand around the back of his neck. "I know that you would."

"I'd do anything for you because I love you."

The thundering of my heart feels like it's going to split my chest in two. "I love you."

He kisses me lightly. It's a loving press against my mouth. "Thank you for being here. Thank you for knowing I needed you here."

"I wouldn't have been anywhere else." I push back to look at him.

Jesus, I love him so much. I wanted to crawl inside his heart last night and hold it together. I wanted to take his pain away and carry it with mine.

"He hated me."

I bite back a rush of tears as I shake my head. "How can anyone hate you?"

"I wasn't his." He moves to roll onto his back, his muscled forearm shielding his eyes. "I'm adopted."

"I know," I say quietly.

He peeks out from under his arm. "You know?"

I motion toward the door. "Your living room is filled with pictures of you and your family. You're like a giant compared to them."

A laugh bursts out of him. "A giant?"

"You're taller than all of them." I laugh too. "You have black hair and beautiful green eyes. They don't."

"How long have you known?"

I shrug. "A long time, I guess. Since the first time I came here and saw the pictures and when I met Kade, I knew for a fact then. He didn't say anything but you two are so different."

He lowers his arm. "Why didn't you say anything?"

I move closer to him so I can run my hand over his chest until I feel the steady beating of his heart. "We never talk about May and Jonas being adopted. Why would we talk about you being adopted? A family is a family and we're all family."

He wraps his strong arms around me and kisses my forehead. "This right here is where I belong."

It's where I belong too. It's where I've always been meant to be.

Chapter 45

Crew

I slide a cup of coffee across the dining room table toward Adley. She took the day off. I didn't ask her to, but I heard her talking to Donovan. She explained that the man she loves lost his father. The words sounded foreign, the pain associated with them even more so.

How do you mourn someone who mourned your existence?

"How was your mom last night?" She asks as she takes a sip from the mug. I made it the way I always do for her, no milk, one cube of sugar and a small spoon next to it, so she can stir it herself.

"She's strong." I cup my hand around my mug. "She'll miss him. They were married a long time."

She swallows hard. "I know you, and your dad weren't close. I mean I assume that you weren't."

I didn't make a secret of the fact that my father wasn't on my list of favorite people. She'd heard me arguing with him on the phone in the past. She's watched me dodge any discussion of him since we met.

"It's still normal to grieve the loss." She glides her hand across the table to touch mine. "Do you want to talk about him?"

"He hated me because I wasn't his," I say it matter-of-factly. "I loved him despite that. Now he's gone."

TROUBLEMAKER   *Deborah Bladon*

She chews on the corner of her lip. "He was the luckiest man in the world."

"How so?" I raise a skeptical brow.

I won't fucking let her make him into a tortured saint who worked hard for his family. He chose work over everything and blood over promise. He was supposed to care for me, and he tried to destroy me instead.

"He got to be your dad, and even if he couldn't see it, that's a privilege that a lot of men would trade almost anything for."

She's too sweet for her own good. I'm grateful that she never met Eli. He didn't deserve the honor of meeting her.

It's fitting that he met Damaris. They were more alike than either would admit. She shoved my birth mother's death in my face whenever she could to break me down, and Eli reminded me of where I came from every opportunity he had.

"He died with a clear conscience." I take a mouthful of the now warm coffee. "I said my peace. He said his. It ended the way it needed to."

She stretches her legs. "What about your birth parents?"

"They've never been up for any parent of the year awards either."

She tosses me a look that says that she knows I'm deflecting the pain with humor. "My birth parents are both dead."

She visibly recoils from that. The cup in her hand shakes. "Both are gone?"

"My birth father died in a car accident. Speed killed him."

TROUBLEMAKER   *Deborah Bladon*

That's all there is to tell. I went to France to track him down since he lived under so many aliases that it took years to rut to the bottom of the pile of fake identities. When I finally did, I was standing in a small graveyard on the outskirts of a charming town outside of Paris staring down at a tombstone with his real name on it.

"What about your birth mother?"

I scrub my hand over my face. It's been years. I've gone to therapy, thrown things against the wall, worked out until my hands bled, and yet the pain is still there whenever I talk about it.

Those conversations only happened with two people outside the safety of the therapist's office I visited weekly for a year after the night my birth mother died.

She wasn't in a comfortable hospital bed with the best care at her disposal. There weren't family members huddled outside the door to her room, willing to do whatever they could to make her last hours more comfortable.

There was me, just me.

"She died in a fire."

Both of her hands leap to her chest. "A fire?"

I could leave it at that and the conversation would be over. It was a tragic death by anyone's standards but more so because her only child refused to help her and left her alone, in a house that was falling apart at the seams with a full bottle of vodka, a package of cigarettes and a lighter.

I nod as I bow my head. "I went to see that afternoon. I took her to a store to get her some food. She wanted that and more."

245

TROUBLEMAKER   *Deborah Bladon*

"More?" Her brows rise. "What do you mean?"

"I gave her everything she needed to set that house ablaze. I gave her every reason not to live."

She stands and takes two large steps until she's in my lap. Her arms wrap around my neck as she presses her cheek to mine. "Don't do that, Crew. Don't blame yourself."

I tuck her closer to me, needing her strength to get the words out. "I hired someone to track her down. They found her in Kentucky."

She nods. "You went to see her?"

"I surprised her." I had to. The woman didn't own a phone. She was renting the house and barely getting by. "She had no idea who I was."

"She must have been in shock."

"She was." I squeeze her closer. "I told her I was her son and she looked at me. She saw the resemblance then. I saw it immediately when she opened the door."

"What happened then?" Her voice is strong and calm. She's everything I'm not right now.

"I offered to buy her dinner but she wanted food from the grocery store, so we went. I had a rental car."

She runs her fingers through my hair. "You took her home after that?"

Swallowing hard, I go on. "We had bags of food and a bottle of cheap booze. I got her the cigarettes she wanted and the lighter she needed."

She taps my shoulder. "I understand."

246

TROUBLEMAKER   *Deborah Bladon*

She does, but she doesn't. It's not as simple as a person dropping a lit cigarette onto a tattered old chair when they're in a drunken haze.

"I asked what else I could do to help her." I stop to kiss her shoulder. She let me dress her in one of my T-shirts and my sweatpants after we made love. I pulled on a pair too before I brought her out here.

"What did she say?" She pulls back to look at me.

"Money. She wanted money."

There's no surprise in her expression. How could there be? I wasn't shocked by the request when it left my birth mother's lips. "What did you tell her?"

"I told her I'd arrange for her to fly back to New York to enter a treatment facility." I look over at my kitchen, where I keep my courage in an aged bottle of scotch that I'm craving. "I promised her a job and a place to live if she cleaned herself up."

Her hand finds my face. "She didn't want that."

"She didn't want that or me," I correct her. "She told me that I should be grateful that she didn't terminate her pregnancy and that she deserved everything I owned for having to put up with me for three years. Then she threw me out and told me to go to hell."

Tears well in the corners of her beautiful blue eyes. "That's so wrong. It's so wrong."

"She died that night," I say matter-of-factly. "In a fire set by a lit cigarette that had fallen onto the chair she was sitting in."

"That's not on you, Crew. You gave her a chance. She didn't take it."

TROUBLEMAKER   *Deborah Bladon*

I know she's right. Nolan has drilled the same words into my brain for years. I held out a hand to the woman who gave me life, she slapped it away and wishing it was different, won't make it so.

TROUBLEMAKER   *Deborah Bladon*

Chapter 46

Adley

I want to smash my hands against something to redirect the pain that I'm feeling. How the hell do people do this? How do they have a child and then treat them worse than a pile of dirt? I don't understand it. I can't comprehend it because my parents have given me nothing but their love and support.

I listen as he talks on the phone to Kade. I can hear the sorrow in his voice, and now I know it's not all about Eli Benton. He's mourning the loss of all of his parents, all of them had a chance to love this incredible man, and they tossed him aside.

I promise myself that the next time I see Pauline Benton, I'm going to hug her and thank her for being exactly what he's always needed.

I saw the affection between them at the hospital the night Eli was admitted. There was as much love in her eyes for him as there is in my mom's eyes when she looks at me. I'm grateful he has that, and I'm glad she has him to lean on.

He ends the call with a brusque, *talk to you later*.

He and Kade have never been close. Their father's death won't change that.

"They'll be a service next week." He tosses his phone on the sofa. "You'll go with me."

It's not a question. He knows I'll be there next to him, holding his hand, holding him up emotionally if need be.

249

TROUBLEMAKER   *Deborah Bladon*

"I need to stop drinking." He scrubs a hand over the back of his neck. "I've done it before. I'm going to try again now."

I'm relieved. I've watched him drink so much scotch in one night that it would level any other man for a week. I've joked about him cutting back in the past, but he's always laughed off those remarks.

"I'll stop drinking too," I offer with a wink. "We'll do it together."

He nods. "You're the best thing that's ever happened to me. I'd go cold sober if that's what you want me to do."

I want him to be healthy and happy.

"We'll replace the liquor with sex." I wiggle my eyebrows. "Whenever you feel the urge to drink, we'll fuck."

He's on me in a flash, his hands tugging down my sweatpants. "I'm thirsty, Ad."

"Me too," I whisper into the stubble on his chin. "From behind? I love it like that."

"Strip now."

He leaves the room on a jog, his heavy steps disappearing down the hallway. I step out of the sweatpants and tug the T-shirt over my head.

"You're the most beautiful woman I've ever seen." He stops in place as soon as he's back in the living room with a condom package in hand. "My breath literally fucking stops when I see you like this. Why did I waste so much time not chasing you?"

I laugh through my tears. He can't know how deeply those words touch me. I'm still reeling from yesterday. The words of the man in the clinic, mixed

TROUBLEMAKER   *Deborah Bladon*

with what Damaris said have played over and over inside of me all day.

I need to tell Crew. I have to hand him my secret the way he handed me his.

He moves closer, shedding his sweatpants with ease as he approaches me. His large hand fists his swollen cock. "From behind and rough, you said?"

I watch as his hand moves to my body, sliding down my navel before it disappears between my legs. "Yes, behind and rough."

He glides his hand over my core. "Your cunt is perfect. You're perfect."

I moan when he slides a finger inside of me. "Like that."

He adds another and then a third as he ups the tempo. I reach back to grab onto anything, but his arm is already wrapped around my waist.

"I'll get you ready like this." His hard cock pulses between us.

I want it now, but he wants more from me first. I drive down onto his hand, circling my hips, taking what I need.

"That's it, beautiful," he whispers against the skin of my neck. "Fuck my hand. Fuck it until you come for me."

I do, and then I bend over the arm of the sofa and come again as he pummels his sheathed length into me with words of love falling from his lips.

***

"I have to go to work." I nestle my head on his chest. "I'm sorry I can't stay with you all day again."

TROUBLEMAKER   *Deborah Bladon*

I want to more than anything, but I heard him telling Nolan on the phone last night that he'd be in the office today. I have a job to do too.

We made love in the living room before we had a long, hot bath together. I took him in my mouth as he stood up to towel dry and with the steam enveloping us, he shot his release on my lips before I licked it as he watched.

He was desperate for more, but we were exhausted. Our bodies sated, our hearts connected and when we got in his bed together, sleep found us quickly.

"Have lunch with me." He doesn't open his eyes. "There's no fucking way I'm going to get through an entire day without kissing you or copping a feel of your tits."

I laugh. "You're feeling better today."

He reaches down to stroke his fingertips over his semi-hard cock as he cracks open one eyelid. "See for yourself how good I feel."

I lick my bottom lip. "You're insatiable."

"Get used to it, woman." His fingers tap dance on my shoulder. "I need to make up for all the years I wasn't fucking you."

"I need to go." I sigh as I stare at him. "You make it hard to walk away."

"You make it hard, period." He strokes the length of his cock. "Tell me the clinic changed its hours and you're clocking in at five a.m."

I let out a tiny laugh. "It's almost nine."

"For fuck's sake," he says in a rough voice. "What are you doing to me? That's twice now that I've overslept by four hours."

TROUBLEMAKER   *Deborah Bladon*

"Maybe your body is telling you that sleep is more important than work." I brush my lips over his. "The world won't crumble if you sleep in once in a while."

"You're more important than anything." He holds me in place. "I'll see you at noon outside the clinic."

"I can't today. There's a staff meeting for all the vet assistants at noon." I kiss him once more before I hop out of bed. "I'll see you tonight back here. I love you, Crew."

His hands fist together on his chest. "My heart is yours, Ad. I love you. I always will."

TROUBLEMAKER   *Deborah Bladon*

Chapter 47

Crew

"How are you doing?" Nolan waltzes into my office. I've been here for a total of ten minutes. I knew he'd make an appearance within the first thirty. "I'm sorry about Eli."

He's not sorry Eli's dead. He's sorry that my chance to have a father died in the hospital bed with him. "I'm all right."

I'm not. How the fuck could I be?

Damaris, my dad's death and then a confessional to Adley.

I have no idea how the hell I'm still upright.

"Ellie sent flowers to Pauline." He sits in one of the chairs in front of my desk. "She doesn't know the whole story since it's never been mine to tell."

I nod in appreciation. I can count on Nolan to be loyal. He knows I would never betray him either.

Since we met, he's always been my brother. We don't speak of our bond often, but we both understand and value it.

"I told Ad I love her."

He leans back in the chair, crossing his ankle over his knee. "That was quick."

He's wrong. It took too long. I've loved her as a friend for close to two years. I've loved her as more for months. "She feels the same way."

"No surprise there." He blinks." Ellie called it a year after you two met. It was the day you set up that date between Adley and Kade."

254

TROUBLEMAKER   *Deborah Bladon*

"Ellie called it back then?" I'm shocked. The last few weeks I've hesitated to talk about Ad around Ellie. I know how protective she is of her best friend. Ellie loves me, but I never believed she would see me as someone who is good for Adley.

"She did. She said you'd end up together. I didn't agree."

I can't help but laugh to myself. "You didn't see it written in the stars?"

He slides forward to rest his palm on the edge of my desk. "I've been by your side for years, Crew. We both know she's as far from your type as there is."

He's right. I know it. "It's easy to have a type when you don't know what you're looking for. I never had to put any thought into it. It was all about convenience then. Now it's different."

"You are in love." He raises both hands in the air. "If I were a betting man, I would have lost big. I never pegged you as the type to settle for one woman."

"It's not settling when the most amazing woman on the planet is in love with you. She loves me, Nolan. Me. How the fuck did that happen?"

"You're not half bad." He smiles. "You're going to be good together."

I push back from my desk. "I'm working half a day today. I'm going to drop by the clinic and surprise Ad, and then I'll spend the afternoon with my mom."

"Take all the time you need." He rounds my desk and waits for me to stand before he tugs me into a hug. "I'm sorry again, Crew. I know it was a shitshow with you and Eli, but the pain has to be there still."

TROUBLEMAKER   *Deborah Bladon*

It is. The day spent with Ad and the last ten minutes with Nolan hasn't lessened it. Time will do that, I hope. I have to let go of my father and the dream that will never come true.

"You know where to find me, pal." He moves to walk out of my office. "Say hi to Ad for me. Tell her we're happy that you came to your senses."

"You're an ass." I shake my head as he leaves. "Tell the kids I miss them."

***

"Hey." I feel a tap on my shoulder just before my hand lands on the handle to the door that leads into Premier Pet Care. "It's like a fucking reunion here today."

I turn around. The guy staring at me is at least a few years younger than me, shaggy blond hair, brown eyes, completely unfamiliar to me. "Who the hell are you?"

"You're Crew Benton." He shoves a fist into my shoulder in some sophomoric college ritualistic greeting.

I slap his hand away and smooth my suit jacket. "I know who I am. Who the fuck are you?"

He holds one hand in front of him palm down, while the other flies in the air like he's taking an oath. "I solemnly swear not to reveal anything about the club or the identities of any of its members."

"Are you high? Drunk? What the fuck is your problem?"

I step to the side and hold open the door when a woman with a dog on a leash exits the clinic.

256

TROUBLEMAKER   *Deborah Bladon*

She gives me a tilt of her chin in appreciation. I toss her back a smile.

"Take off." I move a step closer to the guy who thinks he knows me. He doesn't. It comes with owning a club. Every asshole who you offer a free drink to thinks you're his best friend. It's called marketing, but this kid wouldn't know a good business plan if it bit him in the ass.

"You're here to see her too, aren't you? Did you find her because she's Hale's babe? That's how I found her."

The hair on the back of my neck stands up. Rage races up my spine. "What the fuck did you just say?"

"Adley works here." He drums his fingers over the window that offers a bird's eye view of the street from the reception desk. "I got her name from the tagged posts online. I brought my neighbor's dog down two days ago for some bullshit check up to make sure it was her."

"Step back," I growl. "Move over there."

He does. He walks backward, the entire time his hands are in the front pocket of his ripped jeans. I could deck him on the spot with little blood and no noise.

"She's so fucking hot." He bounces in his tennis sneakers. "Sooner or later she's got to take a break. I've been waiting for over an hour for her to come out."

"Stop talking." I tower over him. "You're going to walk away and never come back. Do you understand me?"

257

TROUBLEMAKER   *Deborah Bladon*

His expression shifts but in an instant that smart-ass grin is back on his mouth. "There's enough to go around."

"Shut the fuck up."

"Those big juicy tits and that smooth pussy." He holds his hands in the middle of his chest as he laughs. "I've jerked off to the memory of that so many times. She's not the kind of chick a man forgets. I didn't get a taste back then, but she's available now, man, so get in line."

I haul him off his feet with my hands on the front of his sweater, pushing him against the wall. "I will fucking ruin your life if you don't shut the hell up."

"You're still defending her?" He pushes against me, but it's futile. I've got at least six inches on him and a good fifty pounds. "That's what got you kicked out of Skyn, man. No piece of ass is worth that."

I stumble back so quickly that he falls to the ground. My stomach churns, my head spins.

There's no fucking way. No. He's so fucking wrong.

"Stay the fuck away from her or I will rip you apart." I spit the words out, but he's already gone, weaving his way through the mid-day crowds of pedestrians.

I haul open the door of the clinic and step inside.

The smells, the sounds, all of it is way too fucking much.

TROUBLEMAKER   *Deborah Bladon*

"Crew? Is that you?" Matilda calls to me from behind the reception desk. "What's wrong? Do you need to sit down?"

"Where is she?" I bark the question out into the air, not bothering to raise my head. "Where is she?"

"Adley?" Her voice nears. I see her white shoes as she steps closer to me. "She's not here. Dr. Hunt told me that she called him and that she wouldn't be in today. That's all I know."

Fuck. How the fuck is this real? She can't be that woman. There is no way in hell Adley is that woman. I would remember her. She would remember me.

Matilda says something else but I'm already halfway out the door with my phone in my palm. I call Ad, it goes directly to voicemail and I curse that fucking club and the arrogant asshole that held her down that night telling her to let herself be used until I smashed my fist through his face.

Chapter 48

Crew

I take another drink straight from the bottle and stare out the window of my apartment at the setting sun. I ran all over this goddamn city for hours looking for Adley. I gave up when I realized that she doesn't want me to find her.

I close my eyes again, but the same memory replays itself on an unending reel.

The sounds of music mixed with fucking coming from the room as I approached the door with Damaris by my side. It was one of our regular nights at Club Skyn.

We'd show up late, fuck other people in the back rooms reserved for members only until the club shut down. Then we'd stagger back here, fall asleep in my bed and I'd be up at the crack of dawn ready to bury myself in work.

That night was different.

We were looking for a woman to play with. Damaris had her type. I had mine.

She scoped out the choices. I watched a crowd of men that had gathered around a table. On the table was a woman, on her back.

I stepped closer to get a better look and heard her soft whimpers right away.

"I need more time. I'm not sure anymore."

One guy was wrapping his cock to ready himself to drive into her. The one standing next to her, with one hand on his dick and the other pinning

TROUBLEMAKER   *Deborah Bladon*

her to the table by her throat, kept telling her to calm down.

"It gets me off. You promised me you'd do this."

She struggled against him, her hands tugging on his wrist, her legs held in place by the guy between them.

I edged closer and looked at her face.

I focused on her eyes. Those goddamn beautiful blue eyes looked at me with a plea I'll never forget.

It wasn't a roleplay. She was terrified.

I pushed the guy between her legs aside before he dove in. He lunged back at me but gave up when I snarled at him. I turned back, and the bastard holding her by her throat told me to fuck off because he was her boyfriend.

He said he made the rules.

"*This is my property,*" he growled at me. "*You can go to fucking hell.*"

My fists flew, his nose broke and his girlfriend slid off the table and disappeared.

I ended my night in the office of the owner, threatening to expose him.

He told me he'd take care of her. He swore he'd change protocol.

I never bothered to step foot in the place again.

I throw the empty bottle of scotch against the wall. It shatters sending a shower of glass everywhere. I drop to my knees and bury my face in my hands.

TROUBLEMAKER   *Deborah Bladon*

Why the fuck didn't I see her face then? I wasted too much of my life without her, and now, I don't know if I'll ever see her again.

***

"Crew." Adley's soft voice whispers in my ear. "I'm here. I'm right here."

I feel her arms circle me from behind. The warmth of her skin caresses my bare back.

"I've got you." She peppers my shoulder with kisses.

I roll over on the floor, my head pounding, my eyes shuttered closed. "Adley."

"Tell me you're all right," she whispers against my mouth.

I reach up and grab her shoulders. The heat from her skin soothes me. "You knew. You knew it was me all along."

She crawls closer to me. Her entire body presses into mine. "I knew."

I know why she didn't tell me. I looked right through her that night. I only saw her fear. I didn't see her face.

I move to sit up, but the fucking room is spinning. I rest my head back down on the cold floor. "I should have killed that bastard. You didn't belong in that place. Why the fuck were you in that place?"

"The same reason you were." Her hand runs over my chest. "I wanted the thrill. I wanted to feel a rush. I wanted more than he could give me."

A deep guttural sound escapes me. It's pained. It's primal. It's uncontrollable. "I was there. I was

TROUBLEMAKER   *Deborah Bladon*

fucking there and didn't see what was right in front of me."

"You see me now," she says through a sob. I feel her tears on my skin. "You love me now."

"I love you. I'll never stop."

She nestles against my chest, her breathing slowing. "When you looked at me that night, I knew you felt my fear. I knew you'd save me."

"I would have torn him apart with my bare hands to get you away from him."

"You did."

"You didn't belong in a place like that." I reach to grab her thigh, to press it against my stomach. "That's not who you are."

"It's who you are," she whispers against my neck. "It's what you like."

"No." I turn to look at her. "I fucked in public because it helped me get off. I will never need that with you."

"Never?"

"Never." I stare in her eyes. The eyes I looked in five years ago when I heard her silent pleas and the eyes I stared into when I fucked her for the first time. "I don't want to share you with anyone, Adley. I don't want anyone to see this." I run my hand over her thigh and up her bare back.

"I'm enough for you."

I love that it's a statement and not a fucking question. "You will always be everything I need."

"Can I take you to bed?" She rolls off me and sits up. The light filtering in from outside frames her like a halo. "I want you to fall asleep in my arms."

TROUBLEMAKER   *Deborah Bladon*

"Carry me there," I joke. "I'm so fucking wasted."

"You have to stop drinking because I need a study partner."

I bolt up into a sitting position. "You need a what?"

"I was accepted into med school today." Her voice trembles. "Sydney called me when the letter arrived. I was on my way to work. I called Donovan and told him about my dream to be a cardiologist. He told me to go home and read the letter and if the news was good to take the day to celebrate."

"Is that why you disappeared? I was trying to find you for hours."

"I thought you were with your mom." She smooths her hand over my brow. "Your dad just died and I know she needs you. I didn't want to interrupt your time with her, so I finally went to see that new apartment my folks moved into three months ago. I've been thinking a lot about them the last few days."

"What did they say about med school?"

"I had every intention of telling you first but I wanted that to be in person."

I smile at her. Of course, she'd want that. She wanted to hold onto that memory.

"My dad started talking about how I needed to make a decision about going back to school to be a vet soon, so I pulled the letter out of my purse, and well, they were happy."

"Happy?" I bark out a laugh." They were over the moon, weren't they?"

TROUBLEMAKER   *Deborah Bladon*

"My dad was over the moon about med school." She presses her lips to mine. "My mom was over the moon that I'm in love."

"That came up?"

"That's what I went over to tell them." She takes a deep breath. "Time flew by, and when I finally looked at my phone in my purse, I saw all your missed calls and a few from Tilly. I tried calling you first, but you didn't pick up so I called her and she told me about the clinic, and the jerk and you. That's when I realized that you knew that I was the girl from the club."

Chapter 49

Adley

He's been asleep for hours. I helped him get to his feet when he said he needed to stand. He leaned on me while we walked to the bedroom. I got in bed with him and held him until he fell asleep and then I slipped out of his arms so I could clean the broken glass.

"It's been one hell of a week." His voice is behind me. "If this is how it's always going to be with us, we need to renegotiate the no drinking policy."

I turn to look at him. He's only wearing his boxer briefs. That's exactly how I left him.

"Next week will be better." I pat the sofa next to me. "I'm going to take you up on your offer."

I watch him stroll toward me. "The one where I asked you to marry me?"

"I haven't heard that one yet." I stare at his face as he lowers himself next to me. "You made an offer when I was putting you to bed."

"Was it to sit on my face? That offer lasts forever."

I slap him on the shoulder. "I will take you up on that offer before I go to work."

He looks out at the darkened sky. "Looks like it will be a multi-hour session."

"You remember the offer, don't you?"

He pats his lap. "Sit here with me."

TROUBLEMAKER   *Deborah Bladon*

I scoot my panty-covered ass across the couch and settle on his lap, my legs straddling his. "Tell me you remember."

"I wish I could remember that night." He presses his index finger to my lips. "I know you don't want to talk about it, but when you do, I'm here."

"Thank you." I kiss the side of his finger. "It's crept back into my life because of the Hale's babe stuff, but I'm getting stronger. I think it's actually helped me to let go of the pain of that night."

"How so?"

"Whenever I thought back about it, I'd see that younger version of myself who was trying too hard to please her boyfriend. I was willing to sacrifice myself to make him happy. I'm not her anymore. I'm strong. I can handle it. It doesn't define who I am. I get to choose what defines me."

"You're right." He runs his hands over my thighs. "You chose to try an experience. It wasn't what you wanted. That doesn't give anyone the right to say a word to you about it."

"I've cried too many tears about it. I don't want to cry anymore."

He looks down at the sofa. "You were crying about it the night we played Truth or Dare."

I nod. "A man sent me a message online and asked if I'd ever been to the Skyn. He saw the picture of Trey and I at Nova, and he thought he recognized me."

"You were at the club more than that one night, weren't you?"

"A half dozen times," I admit." I was mostly in the main club dancing with my boyfriend at the

TROUBLEMAKER   *Deborah Bladon*

time. He took me to the back rooms twice. The first time we watched other people. The second time is when you saw me there."

"A face as beautiful as yours is hard to forget."

"You forgot," I say softly.

"The fire was the week before I saw you there." He's quiet for a moment. So am I. "That's not an excuse for not remembering you. It's definitely not an excuse for the rage I was feeling. I helped you because I had to. I saw the cry for your help in your eye, and there was no way in hell I could ignore it."

I trail my fingertips down his cheek. "When I saw you in Vegas that night when you were offering Ellie a job, I recognized you."

The pad of his thumb runs over my bottom lip. "I'll never forgive myself for wasting these two years, but I'll do everything in my power to make the next seventy the best you've ever had."

"Is that how long we'll be together?"

"God willing." He kisses the corner of my mouth. "I'll spend every single one of those days showing you how much I love you."

"Let's start now." I reach to unbutton the white shirt I'm wearing. It's his, of course. The smell of his skin surrounding me is the reason I put it on when I got out of bed.

He flips me over the same way he did the night we played Truth or Dare.

He hovers above me.

"What will it be, Crew? Truth or Dare?"

"Truth."

TROUBLEMAKER   *Deborah Bladon*

I stare into his pale green eyes. "Will you love me forever?"

"Forever and an extra day." He kisses me softly. "Truth or Dare, Ad?"

"Dare."

A ghost of a smile floats over his sinful mouth. "I dare you to take me up on my offer."

"The one to move in with you?"

He nods. "That one and all the others I'll make until the day I die."

"I'm going to pack up my things tonight." I trace the pad of my thumb over his left brow. "I want to wake up next to you every morning."

"At five a.m."

"Those days are over." I laugh. "Last one, Crew. Truth or Dare?"

"Dare," he answers without missing a beat. "Make it a good one."

"I dare you to make me come."

"You're joking." He rakes my body from head-to-toe. "Add something to that, like within a minute, or with my eyes closed, or with both hands tied behind my back or all of the above."

"With just your kiss," I finish.

"Dare accepted, Dr. York," he growls as he slides down my body. "You never said where the kisses could be."

I arch my back when I feel his breath on my thigh. "You won."

"You better fucking believe I won," he says as he pushes my panties aside to glide his tongue over my core. "I get to be loved by you. There's nothing better in this world than that."

269

Epilogue

Three Years Later

Crew

"Tell your mother what happened at school today." I cross my arms over my chest and stare at my daughter.

Her lips pinch together. She looks at me before her gaze stops on Ad's face. "I told a boy that I didn't like his shoes."

"Megan." I roll my eyes. "You know that's not what I meant."

"I did tell a boy that, dad." She rolls her eyes right back at me. "He has a pair of those shoes that you had to stand in line to buy. Who needs that?"

Adley grins as she looks up from her tablet. "No one needs that."

"Exactly. Mom gets it."

"Megan." I tap my foot on the floor of our new apartment. It's a three bedroom, two blocks from where Adley's parents live. We made the move when we decided to foster a child. Megan was eight then. Now, she's a ten-year-old with an attitude.

I blame May for that. They're in the same class at school. They hang out on the weekends and one afternoon a week Nolan's folks take Megan and May to piano lessons.

Meg loves helping out with baby Emmanuel. He's two-and-a-half now and one of the cutest kids I've ever met.

TROUBLEMAKER   *Deborah Bladon*

We're on the path to adoption. It's a long one, but to have this child as our daughter is worth it. After her mother died when she was three, her grandmother took over the parenting duties. Her death left Megan in the system.

She was shuffled around for two years before she landed in our lives after our home study was complete.

We're a tight trio now. Her love for us has made my wife and me a stronger couple.

I married the love of my life three months after she moved in with me. Our wedding was small. My family was still mourning the loss of my dad, but our vow ceremony started us all on a path to being a more cohesive unit.

It also started me on the road to sobriety. I haven't had a drop since I toasted my bride with a glass of champagne.

I sold the clubs to Kade and cut back on my work at Matiz. I'm in the office from nine-to-five, four days a week and never a minute more.

We spend the holidays out in Westhampton with Adley's folks and the Benton clan.

I have a family now, and a wife who is committed to making her dreams come true.

"What did you do, sweetie?" Ad smiles at Megan. "It can't be worse than all the trouble your dad used to get into."

"When he was a kid?"

Ad shrugs. "Then and last week. He'll always be a troublemaker."

TROUBLEMAKER   *Deborah Bladon*

A laugh bubbles out of Megan. "I told the teacher that he was wrong about how the human heart works, but I didn't get in trouble for it."

My wife puts down the tablet and walks over to where Meg and I are sitting. "Tell me more. How did he say it works?"

Meg reaches for Ad's hands. "He said that it keeps us alive."

Ad settles on the arm of the chair Meg is sitting in. "He's right about that."

"He is, but then someone asked how a baby's heart grows when it's inside its mom."

My beautiful wife pushes a strand of our daughter's red hair from her forehead. "What did the teacher say?"

"He said the baby starts as a bunch of cells and those change into all the parts, like the heart. He said the baby has to be inside its mom for the heart to grow the right way."

I fucking tear up because I know what's coming. I stare at the two most important people in my life, and I start to cry.

"What you did say to that?"

She rests her head on Adley's small baby bump. "I said that my mom is growing my brother's heart inside her belly now, but before I was born, mine grew inside of her heart, even though I was far away."

Ad nods as she tears up. Her fingers touch the middle of her chest. "You're right. It grew right here."

"Will Pauly know I'm his sister when he's born?"

TROUBLEMAKER   *Deborah Bladon*

Paul Benton, my son, will arrive in a little over four months. He shares his name with my mom, who is already buying more baby clothes than he'll ever need.

"Pauly will know it," I say. "He'll look at your face, and he'll say to himself, there she is. That's the girl who will show me the ropes."

"I'll never let anything bad happen to him." She strokes her fingers over Adley's stomach. "I'll teach him everything I know and every night before I go to sleep I'll tell him I love him."

I'll do the same. I'll make sure my son and my daughter both know that I would hang the moon in the sky for them if I could.

I got the woman of my dreams. I have the family I never thought was in my future and I'm living a life that will only get better from here.

I look over at my wife. She's on her way to being a doctor. She's a mother and a daughter. She's also the best friend I'll ever have.

I dared to dream this and now it's my reality. All I have to do now is enjoy every fucking minute of it.

Preview of HUSH

I have three hard and fast rules when it comes to one-night stands.

Don't tell her your last name.

Don't take her home with you.

Don't knock her up.

I'm screwed.

Jane Smith was supposed to be a quick fling. I saw her as a brief escape from the never-ending drama that is my life as a surgeon in New York City.

Now, she's pregnant and scared as hell.

Oh, and apparently her real name is *Chloe Newell.*

It's probably not the best time to tell her that I'm the guy who ruined her life two years ago.

Author's Note: *This romance contains a gorgeous doctor, an unexpected pregnancy and a past connection between the hero and heroine that could change everything. HUSH is part of the Just This Once Series. Each book features a different couple and the books are not connected so they can be read in any order.*

Chapter 1

Evan

"I'm not a coward. I am not a coward." A soft, smooth feminine voice catches me off guard.

I turn toward it and grab a quick glimpse of what looks like the world's most perfect ass in a pair of black lace panties. They vanish the second the woman in question stands upright again, the red umbrella in her hand mangled from the brutal wind.

"You don't strike me as a coward, sweetheart." I raise my near-empty glass of bourbon in a mock toast because any person brave enough to venture out in December in a New York City blizzard dressed like it's the middle of July deserves a medal. This one earns bonus points for having an ass that can halt a snowstorm in its path.

That may or may not be a fact, but the timing is sure as hell spot-on.

The deluge of snow that has blanketed the city for the past five hours has stopped abruptly. That wasn't the case up until a minute ago when I was standing, alone, outside this hotel contemplating what my next move will be.

Big picture stuff, not which-of-my-casual-hookups-should-I-call-tonight stuff.

"Thanks, stranger." She smooths her hands over the short skirt of her frilly navy blue dress as she takes in the length of my six foot plus frame. "I'm not your sweetheart, though."

Wheat blonde hair, hazel eyes, glossy full pink lips, and an attitude.

Forget the big picture. My next move needs to involve this woman.

My eyes don't leave her angelic face even though I want to trail my gaze and my mouth over every inch of her body. "Fair enough. Introduce yourself, and while you're at it, I'd love to meet your imaginary friend too."

I can't resist the urge to look when her nipples furl into hard points beneath the airy fabric of her dress. As much as I want that reaction to be from the rich baritone of my voice, I suspect it's from the burst of wind that just picked up her skirt. There's a brief flash of sheer lace covering smooth skin before she yanks the hem of the skirt back in place.

My evening just got a whole hell-of-a-lot better.

"My imaginary friend?" She tucks a piece of her windswept hair behind her ear. My fist clenches in envy. I want those waves balled in my hand so tightly that the only noise she makes is one that tells me she wants my cock deeper.

I crack a smile. "You were hell bent on convincing someone that you're not a coward. Since we're the only two out here and there's no phone in your hand, I take it that your imaginary friend is the asshole who thinks you're a coward. I'll argue your case if you point me in his direction, or is it her direction?"

"Are you a lawyer?"

I'll be anything she wants me to be. I'm a surgeon, vascular to be precise, and I have to be.

Tonight, I don't want to be Dr. Evan Scott. I'd rather be the star of her future fantasies; that one awe-inspiring lay all women look back on for the rest of their life when they get themselves off.

"Not guilty." I hold my hand up in mock surrender. "Your name, beautiful. What is it?"

Her thickly lashed eyes widen as the heavy metal awning above us creaks under the weight of the wet snow. "It's Jane. Jane Smith."

She's the third *Jane Smith* I've met this month.

I'm not offended that the name offered is as fake as the smile plastered on the face of the doorman who is watching our every move from the warm comfort of the lobby. Experience has taught me that women in this town hide behind a false persona for just three reasons.

One is that their wedding ring is tucked in a pocket or a purse and they don't want the night to seep into their two kids, bake sales, walking the dog in the park, day-to-day life.

For the record, I avoid those women at all costs. They're easy to spot, even if they think they're fooling everyone, including themselves.

The second reason women morph into Jane Smith, Jane Doe or just plain Jane is they're prepping to hand over a fake number.

Eye contact is everything, and if a woman I'm after can't make it with me, I tap out. There are too many women on this island who are interested in what I'm offering. I'm not into wasting my time on someone whose type isn't tall with dark brown hair, blue eyes, muscular pecs, that cut V that women dream of, and a thick nine-inch cock.

Yeah, I measured. Every man does. He's a fucking liar if he doesn't admit it.

The third reason is why my new blonde friend tossed out the name Jane Smith to me just now. She's looking for the same thing I am. One night of no-personal-details, uninhibited, I-dare-you-to-walk-straight-after-that fucking.

"It's nice to meet you, Jane." I extend a hand because in public I'm always the perfect gentleman.

She takes a step forward, dragging her sorry looking umbrella behind her. Her hand lands in mine for a soft shake. It's just enough pressure to stir my cock. "What's your name, stranger?"

I could easily be the Jack to her Jane, but I want to hear my name from those lips tonight. "Evan."

The look on her face is all surprise and awe like I've already got two fingers inside her and I'm honed in on that spot that will etch my name into her memory forever. "Is that your real name?"

I crane my neck to look at the lobby. The last thing I need right now is for anyone I work with to breeze past us and call me *Dr. Scott.* I have to get this woman into a hotel room and out of that dress now.

"According to my driver's license, it is." I circle the pad of my thumb on her palm before I let her hand go. "I'm going inside to refill my drink and then I'm heading upstairs. Can I get you anything, Jane?"

She reaches up to touch her neck. It's a subtle sign that she wants my hand, or maybe my mouth, there. "Are you inviting me up to your room?"

Technically, I'm inviting her to a room I haven't rented yet. I was out here catching a breath of frigid nor'easter air. I did my time inside when I took the podium, ran through an off-the-cuff speech about the boatload of accolades my boss acquired in his career and then handed him a silver wristwatch courtesy of his wife. He threw the goddamn shindig on his own dime and then expected me to kiss ass in public to hold onto a job I'm not sure I want.

"If you are, I'm game," Jane tosses that jewel out before I have a chance to offer a formal invitation to get naked with me. "I didn't notice you at the ceremony. Are you a friend of the bride or the groom?"

It's the obvious conclusion to jump to. I'm dressed in a tuxedo. There's a wedding reception in the ballroom tonight. She has no clue that I was just in the hotel's five-star restaurant with a group that consists of primarily sixty-something-year-old surgeons all desperate to one-up each other with elaborate descriptions of their summer homes.

At thirty-four I'm the baby of the bunch, hence the reason I'm standing in the bitter cold with a drink in my hand contemplating why I went to medical school in the first place.

Jane marches on, nerves twitching at the edge of her words. "I'm a friend of Leanna. I'm actually one of her bridesmaids. I had to get the hell out of there when Henry started talking about how committed he is to her. It's bullshit. You know that, don't you? He totally screwed her over this past summer when he was in Vegas. She forgave him and now they're married. Can you believe that?"

"Henry is a selfish son-of-a-bitch."

Her eyes flick up to meet mine. "What's your room number?"

The snow starts again, large flakes of unwanted inconvenience. I need a condom. My gaze darts up and down the street. Other than a restaurant a block over, every other storefront and business are locked up tight.

Late Sunday night will do that to Manhattan. A snowstorm doesn't help.

"You have protection, right?" Pretty Jane reads my mind like a sensual sorceress. "I didn't bring any condoms with me."

Normally, I'd have at least a few tucked in my pocket, but I got dressed at the hospital. An emergency surgery this afternoon cut into my prep time for this hellish evening, so I had my rental tux delivered. I changed in the locker room and forgot one of the essentials. The breath mints made it into my pants pocket next to my wallet, but the condoms didn't.

Fucking great.

I'm not sending this woman on a mission to get me a rubber. That comes with the risk of her bailing on me because she doesn't see the effort as worth the reward.

It's worth it, in spades, or in her case, orgasms.

"I've got that covered, or should I say, it will be covered," I quip with a tip of my glass before I down the last swallow. I'll go floor-by-floor and door-to-door in this hotel to find a condom if need be. "Do you need to say goodbye to Leanna before you bail?"

She blows an adorable puff of air out from between her lips. "I do. I left my purse in there. What about you?"

"I didn't have a purse that matched my outfit tonight," I joke. "I'll meet you in the lobby in thirty minutes. We can head up to the room together."

"Make it fifteen," she counters, a challenge woven into her tone. "I'll take a London Fog."

"Consider it done," I whisper as she breezes past me, the maimed umbrella dragging behind her. The doorman jumps into action and props open the heavy glass door. Jane steps into the vestibule just as the ugly winter wind gives not only me but the doorman, the early holiday gift of an eyeful of her luscious ass.

Something tells me this night is going to be one for the record books.

Coming soon

Preview of WORTH

A Two-Part Novel Duet

I notice him immediately. It's impossible not to. Julian Bishop is the man of the hour, after all. This celebration, complete with expensive champagne and stiff-backed wait staff, has drawn the crème de la crème of Manhattan's social elite. It's the place to be tonight, and with a lot of crafty manipulation and a fair bit of luck, I'm standing in the midst of it, wearing a killer little black dress and diamond earrings I borrowed from a broker who has sold more than her fair share of apartments with Park Avenue addresses.

"I got you another glass of champagne, Maya."

I turn toward my date for the evening, taking the tall crystal flute from his hand. I enjoy a small sip while I look at his hands. They're adequate, not too large, and not too small. Those hands, along with the brief kiss he gave me when he picked me up tonight promise a night of passion that would be forgettable at best. He's nothing to write home about or to write about at all, for that matter.

"Thanks, Charlie," I purr. "Where's your drink?"

He nudges the sexy-as-all-hell, black-rimmed glasses up his nose with his index finger. He has a nerd with a side of male model look. That's what made me stop at his desk two weeks ago to ask if I could borrow his stapler.

I don't staple. If I did, I'm sure I'd find one in my desk, hidden underneath the three dresses and two pairs of shoes I have tucked in the drawer. I never know when a change of wardrobe is called for. A girl has to be ready for anything when she's trying to claw her way up the hierarchy of the Manhattan real estate market.

"I had one. That's my limit." He squints as he looks at the bar. "Is she here yet? I heard someone say she's going to make an entrance."

I heard someone say she's a dirty, dirty slut.

That someone was me. I said it to myself. She's far from dirty or slutty. She's a lawyer, Harvard educated, with looks to rival her brains. Jealousy is a filthy accessory and I don't wear it well at all.

"I don't think she's arrived." I turn back to where Julian's standing. He looks identical to the way he did when I first laid eyes on him. That was a year ago. I was helping a friend and he was offering her a job. Our paths crossed, the energy flowed and then he left. I never saw the man again.

I would have settled for one tumble in the sheets of his bed. A brief encounter would have satisfied my craving but it wasn't meant to be. He continued on his happily-ever-path and I swam the dating waters of Manhattan occasionally snagging a Charlie in my net.

"I'm going to mingle," I say it like I mean it. "I'll meet you back here in thirty."

Charlie looks down at his watch. It's not impressive. That's not Charlie's style.

"Thirty minutes, Maya." He touches the lenses of his glasses with two of his fingers before he points them right at me. "I'm going to have my eye on you."

Good for you, Cowboy.

I take my champagne, my spirit of adventure and my too tight black heels and I walk across the room. I took my time getting dressed tonight just for that one split second that we all live for. It's that moment when the man you imagine running naked through a field of daisies with or fucking in a back alley, turns and looks at you.

I've been planning this for two months.

Plotting every word I'll say when his eyes meet mine. I'm counting on him remembering me because I've been told I'm not easy to forget.

"Maya Baker." The voice behind me is unmistakably his. Warm with a hint of control, deep with a promise of pleasure.

I start to pivot at the sound of it. It's a beacon, a pull that is too strong to resist.

"Don't turn around." A hand, steady and determined, rests on my hip. The fingertips assert enough pressure to control my movement. "I don't recall seeing your name on the guest list."

Something's caught Julian's cock's attention. I can feel it pressing against me in the middle of this crowded room while we wait for his business partner, rumored lover and person I'd most like to lock in a closet for eternity to arrive. "I was a last minute addition."

"A welcome addition," he adds. "Are you enjoying yourself?"

I feel the undercurrent of desire. It was there last year when we met. It's stronger now.

"I am now." I push my fingers into his on my hip.

His chest lifts and falls. "I'm needed on the stage. You won't run away before we have a chance to talk, will you?"

I turn my head to look up at him. Black hair, ocean blue eyes and a face that would make any woman lock her office door to imagine a moment alone with him.

I've done it. Many women in Manhattan have.

"You're as handsome as ever, Julian."

He rounds me, his hand still holding mine. "You're more enchanting than the day we met, Maya. I've followed your career. I have a position I think you'd be interested in."

Coming soon

THANK YOU

Thank you for purchasing my book. I can't even begin to put to words what it means to me. If you enjoyed it, please remember to write a review for it. Let me know your thoughts! I want to keep my readers happy.

For more information on new series and standalones, please visit my website, www.deborahbladon.com. There are book trailers and other goodies to check out.

If you want to chat with me personally, please LIKE my page on Facebook. I love connecting with all of my readers because without you, none of this would be possible.
www.facebook.com/authordeborahbladon

Thank you, for everything.

ABOUT THE AUTHOR

Deborah Bladon has never read a romance hero she didn't like. Her love for romance novels began when she was old enough to board the bus, library card in hand to check out the newest Harlequin paperbacks. She's a Canadian by heart, and by passport, but you can often spot her in New York City sipping a latte and looking for inspiration for her next story. Manhattan is definitely her second home.

She cherishes her family and believes that each day is a gift for writing, for reading, and for loving.

Printed in Poland
by Amazon Fulfillment
Poland Sp. z o.o., Wrocław